The Stolen Show

Read all the mysteries in the

NANCY DREW DIARIES

Nancy Drew DIARIES™

The Stolen Show

#18

CAROLYN KEENE

Aladdin

NEW YORK   LONDON   TORONTO   SYDNEY   NEW DELHI

ALADDIN

An imprint of Simon & Schuster Children's Publishing Division

1230 Avenue of the Americas, New York, New York 10020

First Aladdin paperback edition September 2019

Text copyright © 2019 by Simon & Schuster, Inc.

Cover illustration copyright © 2019 by Erin McGuire

Also available in an Aladdin hardcover edition.

For information about special discounts for bulk purchases, please contact Simon & Schuster Special Sales at 1-866-506-1949 or business@simonandschuster.com.

The Simon & Schuster Speakers Bureau can bring authors to your live event. For more information or to book an event contact the Simon & Schuster Speakers Bureau at 1-866-248-3049 or visit our website at www.simonspeakers.com.

Series designed by Karin Paprocki

Cover designed by Heather Palisi

Interior designed by Mike Rosamilia

The text of this book was set in Adobe Caslon Pro.

Manufactured in the United States of America 0819 OFF

2 4 6 8 10 9 7 5 3 1

Library of Congress Cataloging-in-Publication Data

Names: Keene, Carolyn, author.

Title: The stolen show / by Carolyn Keene.

Description: First Aladdin hardcover/paperback edition. | New York : Aladdin, 2019. | Series: Nancy Drew diaries ; #18 |

Summary: While investigating a case of sabotage at a dog show, Nancy and her friends are drawn into an undercover international operation in pursuit of a jewel smuggler.

Identifiers: LCCN 2018037376 (print) | LCCN 2018043894 (eBook) |

ISBN 9781534405790 (eBook) | ISBN 9781534405776 (pbk) | ISBN 9781534405783 (hc)

Subjects: | CYAC: Dog shows—Fiction. | Sabotage—Fiction. | Robbers and outlaws—Fiction. | Mystery and detective stories.

Classification: LCC PZ7.K23 (eBook) | LCC PZ7.K23 Sto 2019 (print) | DDC [Fic]—dc23

LC record available at https://lccn.loc.gov/2018037376

Contents

Dear Diary,

WINTER BREAK IS ALWAYS AN EXCITING time of year, but this one looks like it's going to be extra special. The girls and I have been invited on an all-expenses-paid trip to Quebec City in Canada to participate in a regional dog show! We'll get to stay in a fancy hotel, visit the winter carnival, and hang out with some real canine champions. It's going to be so amazing to get on a plane and fly away from River Heights for a while. Surely the excitement of a dog show will still be more relaxing than my usual schedule of fighting crime and solving mysteries— won't it?

The Stolen Show

CHAPTER ONE

A Winter Wonderland

FROM WHERE I SAT IN THE FRONT SEAT OF the taxi, I was the first to get a full view of the banner that arched over the old cobblestoned street, reaching from one colorful building to another. In festive red letters, it read BIENVENUE AU CARNAVAL DE QUÉBEC! Up ahead, I could see crowds of people milling through the streets, swaddled in winter coats and hats, their hands filled with plates of food or steaming cups of hot drinks. A light dusting of snow was sprinkled over everything, giving the whole of Quebec City the look of a picturesque sculpture in a snow globe, just waiting to be shaken up.

"Look at this place!" George exclaimed from the back seat, leaning between the front seats to get a look out the windshield. She pulled her smartphone out of the pocket of her practical red winter parka and began snapping photos of the scene. "You guys, we have to stop and grab something to eat from one of these shops before we head to the hotel. My kingdom for poutine."

"Poutine?" Bess asked. Bess and George are cousins. They're both my best friends, and the three of us are virtually inseparable.

Bess's fair skin was still flushed from waiting outside in the cold for our taxi from the airport into town. She probably should have worn something a little warmer than her knitted beret and ivory peacoat, but Bess always was more fashionable than she was practical. She smoothed down her long blond hair, calming the flyaway strands thrown up by the wind. "What's poutine?"

"Only the most delicious thing in the world," George answered, her dark brown eyes sparkling. "It's french fries and cheddar cheese curds drenched in gravy."

"That sounds a little . . . ," Bess began delicately, "heavy."

"Don't knock it till you've tried it," George countered. "Have I ever steered you wrong?"

Bess's eyebrow quirked. "Ahem—haggis!" she said, pretending to cough.

"What? Haggis is good!" George spluttered.

"If you like spicy oatmeal made of meat," I muttered with a smirk.

George smacked her hand against her chest in mock dismay. "*Et tu*, Nancy?"

"Don't worry," I said with a laugh. "I'll try the poutine. We both will—isn't that right, Bess?"

"Oh, all right," Bess said. "But right now, I'd much rather have a hot cocoa. How long before you're supposed to meet Louise at the hotel, Nancy?"

I checked my watch. It was only a quarter past ten, and I wasn't expected at Château Frontenac until eleven. "We've got plenty of time. Why don't we get out here and walk? We don't have a lot of baggage to carry, and we can pick up a snack on the way."

"Sounds perfect!" George replied, pulling the furry hood over her short, dark hair. "Forty-five minutes to stuff ourselves with Canadian delights before Nancy goes to the dogs."

I chuckled and pulled out some Canadian bills to pay the driver. It was, in fact, dogs that had brought the three of us to Quebec City. A week ago my father got a frantic call from an old friend of his, Louise Alain. She used to work for him as a paralegal many years ago before moving back to Quebec, where she grew up, to raise show dogs. Louise had slipped on a patch of ice outside her house and broken her ankle. But that wasn't the real problem: the biggest dog show of the year was coming up in a week, and she couldn't walk! She desperately needed someone to step in and be her show dog's handler, or else she'd have to drop out of the show. I had recently learned that "handler" was the term used to describe the person who guides show dogs around the arena during competitions. Unfortunately, Louise's backup handler had been stricken with the flu, and her options were slim. So she was calling in an old favor, hoping her old boss's daughter might be willing to take a free vacation in exchange for a couple of days' work. Being that we were already on a winter holiday from school—and that she was willing to pay for George and Bess as well, so I wouldn't have to travel alone—I was only too happy to oblige! I didn't know the first thing about being a dog handler, of course, but Louise assured me over the phone that she would teach me everything I needed to know. "You always had a way with animals," Louise had said. "I'm sure you'll do great!"

Still, as I got out of the car and felt the first blast of cold Canadian air on my face, I realized that it wasn't the only thing making me shiver. Bess must have noticed my expression as we pulled our bags from the trunk of the taxi. "Oh, Nancy, you're not nervous, are you?" she asked.

"I mean . . . a little bit," I answered truthfully. "Being in front of huge crowds of people isn't my favorite thing in the world."

"Nance, you need to relax and have fun," George exclaimed, slapping me on the back. "Look where we are! If you can handle a constant parade of criminals, saboteurs, and petty thieves, you can handle walking a bull terrier around in a big circle. What's the worst that could happen?"

I smirked. "George," I said, "did you forget who you're talking to? I think that statement could probably be filed under Famous Last Words."

It was true—nothing is ever quite so simple when you're an amateur detective with a penchant for attracting trouble everywhere you go. But George was right about one thing: we were in a winter wonderland, so the best thing I could do right now was enjoy it.

We found ourselves standing on Rue Saint Louis, just under the shadow of a beautiful stone bridge. The bridge boasted domed towers and a crenelated archway that looked like it should be part of an ancient castle. To our left, in a large clearing dotted with trees, some carnival goers were wandering into a modern-looking building made entirely of ice, while nearby a crowd cheered on two teams of young athletes playing a competitive game of hockey.

"This is amazing," Bess said, her blue eyes taking it all in. "There's so much to see!"

"I know, right?" George replied. "That's the annual ice palace over there—it's where Bonhomme lives. We've got to go visit before we leave!"

"Who's Bonhomme?" I asked.

"He looks kind of like a snowman wearing a red hat," George replied. "He's like the king of the carnival. He's supposed to be the spirit of happiness, who brings the spring after winter."

"Well then, we'd better get a selfie with him," Bess said seriously. "You know, for the flowers."

We walked on, enjoying the wondrous sights and smells of the carnival. The attractions, the shops, the restaurants, the beautiful stone buildings lining the streets . . . it was like a storybook! George got her poutine—which, I will admit, was delicious—and Bess got her hot cocoa. I ended up buying something called a beaver tail, which tastes a lot better than it sounds. It's actually a warm, tail-shaped pastry topped with cinnamon sugar. By the time I was done eating it, I had forgotten all about being nervous.

After wandering around for about fifteen minutes in a sugar-and-gravy-induced haze, I finally stopped and realized that we were quite a ways from where we had started. My watch read 10:50 a.m. *Darn,* I thought. *I lost track of time. Now we have only ten minutes to get to the hotel, or I'm going to be late!* "George," I said. "We need to be at the château ASAP! What's the fastest route from here?"

George handed me the remnants of her poutine and pulled out her phone, poking at it until a map appeared on the screen. "Let's see here," she muttered, squinting at the unfamiliar streets.

Up ahead, I watched as a well-dressed woman with ash-blond hair and sunglasses rounded a corner. "I can't," she was saying into the phone at her ear. "I've got to get Daisy ready for the show, and—"

"George, watch where you're going!" Bess called out.

But it was too late. Both distracted by their phones, George and the woman collided. They stumbled, and the phones went flying. I winced as they hit the ground with an unpleasant *slap*.

"Oh!" George stammered, reddening. "I'm so sorry!"

"That's quite all right," the woman said with a quick, reassuring smile. "These things happen." She went to reach for her phone, but I was standing closer to where they had fallen.

"Please," I said, "allow me!" I bent to pick up the phones from the sidewalk, and luckily, it looked like they had both managed to survive the fall without much damage. The screen of the woman's phone displayed a photograph of a smiling family—a handsome man, two young girls in matching dresses, and a large black-and-tan Doberman pinscher, posing for the photo with its pointy ears up and its head cocked in curiosity.

I dusted the phone off with my sleeve and handed it back to the woman. "What a lovely family!" I said. "Though I might have expected 'Daisy' to be a poodle, not a Doberman!"

The woman froze and took her sunglasses off to see me more clearly. Her eyes were startlingly blue. "How did you—?" she started to ask.

I blushed. "Sorry," I apologized. "I couldn't help but hear you talking about getting 'Daisy ready for the show,' and since there's a big dog show this weekend, I just put two and two together. I didn't mean to be nosy."

"She can't help it," George added with a grin. "Telling Nancy not to pry is like telling the earth to stop revolving around the sun."

The suspicious expression dropped from the woman's face, and she laughed. "Well, you certainly are observant, young lady! And here I thought you were some kind of crazed stalker or something. What a relief!"

"Do crazed stalkers normally go after show-dog handlers?" Bess asked.

The woman raised an eyebrow. "Stranger things have happened at Westminster, let me tell you!" she replied. "Are you ladies here for the dog show as well, or the winter carnival?"

"Both, really," I answered. "We just flew in from River Heights to be here! I'm going to be taking over as the handler for my friend's dog. She hurt her ankle last week and can't do it herself. Her name is Louise Alain. Do you know her?"

"I know of her, certainly," the woman said, chuckling. "Everyone does. Louise has quite the reputation among dog show enthusiasts. I'm not surprised she's importing a handler from across the border—the woman simply never gives up. She's quite amazing. Although I think you'll find that most people in the business of showing dogs are quite unique, each in their own way. Just like the dogs themselves!" She sighed and smiled to herself. "Honestly, I just adore doing the shows. It gets me out of the house, meeting new people—although I do miss my little ones while I'm gone." She glanced down at the picture on her phone, her blue eyes soft. "Annabelle and Eleanor. Aren't they the sweetest?"

"Very sweet," I said, as Bess cooed over the picture. George nodded vaguely—she wasn't a big fan of little kids in general. They tended to make her nervous.

The woman noticed George's reticence and laughed. "Oh, honey," she said. "You haven't been bitten by the mommy bug yet, have you? You're so young—you'll get there! And then you'll want to hold babies all the time!"

"Um," George said, paling.

Suddenly the woman clapped herself on the head in dismay. "Goodness, how rude of me! Here I am, chatting up a storm, and I haven't even introduced myself." She stuck out her hand with a wink. "I'm Helen Bradley—it's been lovely bumping into you."

The three of us introduced ourselves in turn, and Helen was kind enough to direct us to the hotel. She and the rest of the dog owners and handlers were staying there too. Then Bess reminded us that we were already running late, so we quickly excused ourselves.

"Sorry to run off, but we've got to go!" I said. "Maybe we'll see you later?"

"I'm sure you will, ladies!" Helen replied with a cheery wave. "In the meantime, enjoy the city!"

"Ugh," George muttered as we hurried away. "If

you guys ever see a mommy bug coming to bite me, please let me know so I can squash it."

"Oh, come on, George," said Bess, giving her cousin a playful nudge. "She was so nice!"

"Yeah, she was nice," George admitted. "But that is the type of lady who will make you sit through a slideshow of her baby's first everything. Better that we got out while we could!"

"Run now, bicker later!" I commanded. We jogged through the streets, wheeling our suitcases behind us and dodging tourists. We arrived at the hotel with only moments to spare.

The Château Frontenac had to be one of the most beautiful buildings I had ever seen. It stood a little above the rest of the city, like a shining castle on a hill, surrounded by skeletal trees made cheerful by a dusting of snow. There was a tall central structure with domes and spires, and the rest of the hotel was built around it in a square that boasted turrets and towers, which looked like they were protecting the inner building. The whole hotel was made of cream and golden brick, with sage-green metal rooftops, and hundreds of windows providing guests a show-stopping view of the city beyond. The girls and I grinned at one another, giddy with excitement, before rolling our suitcases into the lobby.

Inside, everything was gold, crystal, and light. The doors and elevators glistened, reflecting the warm yellow glow of the chandeliers above. The air had the dark, comforting smell of wood polish, and I took a moment to breathe it all in.

"Well, well, well," a voice said from a few feet away. "Nancy Drew! The last time I saw you, young lady, you were knee-high to a grasshopper. Look at you now!"

I turned to see a sturdy-looking older woman with short, curly brown hair grinning wolfishly at me from a love seat, her foot encased in a medical boot.

"Louise!" I exclaimed, walking over to embrace her. Louise lurched to her feet and gave me a stunningly strong hug before pulling away to do the same for both Bess and George, who each sputtered a breathless greeting while Louise gleefully crushed their ribs.

"Thank you for coming, Red," Louise said with feeling, using an old nickname that referred to the reddish blond color of my hair. "You saved my butt, you really did. I'd have been up a creek if you hadn't!"

"Anything for one of Dad's old friends," I replied. "And anyway, how could I turn down a free vacation with my friends?"

"How was your trip, girls?" Louise asked, turning to them.

"Well," Bess began. "The flight was a little delayed because of a storm coming up from the south, but—"

"Oh, good," Louise said, clapping her hands with finality and rubbing them together. "We've got a lot of prep to do for this show, and there's no time to waste! As soon as you check in and put away your luggage, we're off to the convention center to practice. We just need to wait for Marge. . . ."

"Marge?" George asked. She looked dizzy from the speed at which Louise seemed to live her life. "Who's Marge?"

"My bully, of course!" Louise replied. "Ah, there she is now!"

We turned to see a pure white bull terrier striding into the lobby, being led by a porter. "Thank you, Genevieve," Louise said to the porter, taking the leash from her hand. Louise had written to say that she was checking into the hotel a few days early "to get the lay of the land." Seemed to me she was already ruling this land. Marge sat on her haunches and regarded us with her small, dark eyes. Like all bull terriers, she had a long, flat head and a muscular body.

Bess, instantly smitten, knelt down in front of Marge and began rubbing her behind the ears. "Oh, aren't you just the most adorable puppy on earth?" she cooed. "Aren't you?"

"Careful," Louise chuckled. "You keep going like that, she'll never leave you alone."

George and I introduced ourselves to Marge with some pats and ear scratches as well. For her part, Marge sniffed my hand intensely before leaning in and giving me a very long and slobbery lick across the face.

"Ah, good, she likes you," Louise noted with approval. "Can't have her despising her new handler, can we? Now, go check in. Marge and I will meet you girls back here in fifteen minutes." She took up the crutch leaning against the table in front of her and hopped toward a comfortable chair.

The three of us checked in, stowed our luggage in our rooms, and quickly freshened up. We got down to the lobby just in time to hear Louise asking the porter to call a taxi to the convention center.

A few minutes later, with Marge leading the way, we piled into the taxi and took a short ride to the nearby convention center, a large, modern building made mostly of glass. We walked inside, where dogs of every imaginable size and variety were there with their owners, checking out the numerous vendor tables that were set up in the lobby. While the people pursued jewel-encrusted collars and hand-painted pet portraits, the dogs sniffed at jars of treats and one another's rear ends with interest. Louise hobbled in like she owned the place, and immediately accosted a petite, middle-aged woman with deep brown skin and red-framed eyeglasses.

"Angie, my girl!" Louise said, clapping the woman on the back with her free hand.

Over black leggings, Angie wore a bright red sweatshirt that was covered in paw prints and read DOGS ARE MY FAVORITE PEOPLE. She had been engaged in conversation with a tall blond man who was impeccably dressed in a light gray blazer and slacks.

"*Voyons donc*, Louise!" Angie sputtered, rubbing her shoulder where Louise's hand had landed. "Is it impossible for you to say hello to me without leaving me in tatters?"

"Clearly not," the blond man said, brushing an invisible speck of grit off his sleeve.

"Oh, I'm sorry, old girl," Louise replied. "I'm just so excited! Here's my new handler: the young Miss Nancy Drew! I'm here to show her and her friends the ropes. Girls, this is my very best friend, Angie Wilson." Louise glanced at the gentleman next to her. "And the fancy boy next to her is Chuck Dubois. He's all right."

She pronounced the name "Doo-boys," which seemed to make Mr. Dubois wince.

"Charles, *s'il vous plaît*," the man said, shaking our hands. "Miss Alain is fond of nicknames, but me, I am less so."

"And who is this handsome fellow with you?" Bess asked, looking at Charles's dog. The dog was almost the same color as his owner's blazer and sat on its haunches, watching the crowd with a sort of detached amusement.

Charles's face brightened. "Ah, *oui*, this is my Weimaraner, Coco Diamonds Are Forever."

George gave a long whistle. "Wow," she said. "That's quite a name!"

"She's quite a dog," Charles replied.

"A lot of the show dogs have very complex names," Angie explained. "Oftentimes the names reflect the dog's credentials or pedigrees, or sometimes they just help breeders distinguish one litter of pups from another."

Louise huffed. "Nope," she said, crossing her arms.

"Just 'Marge' is enough for me. Her quality speaks for itself."

"Or at least her owner certainly does," Charles murmured.

Louise raised her eyebrow at him. "Someone needs a muzzle over there," she said. "And it isn't the Weimaraner."

I leaned over to whisper in Angie's ear. "Are they always this . . . hostile?"

Angie nodded. "It's just their way. Don't worry—they're all bark and no bite."

"Where's your dog, Angie?" Bess asked, stepping over to us.

"Oh—Marshmallow Fluff is just having a snooze in her crate. I'll take you to her!"

Angie led us to a side area, past a checkpoint, where lines of dog crates stood. As we walked, George turned back to me and mouthed, *Marshmallow Fluff?!* I smiled and shrugged. The dog names certainly were entertaining!

"Here she is," Angie said, stopping at a very large

crate in the corner. "Wakey, wakey, Marshy! You've got some fans who want to meet you. . . ." She knelt down to open the door to the crate and look inside. A moment passed as Angie reached inside, the expression on her face changing from excitement to horror.

"Oh!" Angie cried out.

"What?" I said, suddenly alert. "What is it? Is your dog okay?"

"She's breathing," Angie said, her face suddenly pale. "But she won't wake up! I think she's been drugged!"

❧

CHAPTER TWO

A Sticky Situation

ANGIE'S ANGUISHED CRY ATTRACTED THE attention of many of the other attendees, who quickly congregated around us as we pulled Marshmallow Fluff from her crate. She was an Old English sheepdog with a fluffy gray-and-white coat—exactly like the dogs in numerous stories and movies from my childhood. She was alarmingly limp, with a line of drool seeping from her open mouth—but Angie was right, her breathing was deep and steady. Angie was on her knees beside me but seemed paralyzed by the sight of her beloved pet laid low.

"What happened?" a deep voice asked. I looked up to see a large man with copper-brown skin and wavy black hair watching us with concern.

"Is she going to be all right?" a woman asked.

"I think so," I said loudly. "But please back up, everybody, and give her some air!" The crowd took two steps back, and I rubbed Marshmallow's head. "C'mon, girl," I murmured, glancing back at her owner's ghostly pallor. "Wake up! Angie needs you!"

After a few tense moments, Marshmallow let out a deep groan and began to stir. Her head and legs twitched, as if she were waking from a terrible dream— and then, finally, she opened her eyes.

The big dog stared at me for a moment, and then turned back to Angie. Then, like a small child calling for its mother, she whined. Angie wrapped her arms around Marshmallow's head, her eyes blurry with tears. "Oh, my sweet puppy! You're all right! Oh, I was so scared!" Marshmallow seemed to understand her owner's distress and helpfully licked the tears off her face.

After a moment, Angie pulled away, a confused look on her face. Something pink was stuck to her hand, tendrils of it trailing back to Marshmallow's flank. "Wh-what . . . ?" Angie stammered. "What is this?"

I followed the tendrils and discovered a wad of pink goop stuck in the dog's thick fur. I picked at it, but it was stuck fast, and only stretched as I pulled. I sniffed my fingers and immediately recognized the cloying, sweet smell. "Bubble gum," I said. "And it looks like it's not the only piece." Angie and I inspected the dog further and found more and more pieces—ten in total.

"This is terrible," Angie said. "It's going to be nearly impossible to remove all of this from Marshmallow's fur. I'll have to cut it out. . . . Her perfect coat will be ruined." She covered her face with her hands.

George and Bess approached, and I got up to stand next to them. "What do you think, Nancy?" Bess asked.

I crossed my arms over my chest and sighed. "I think someone must have given Marshmallow a drugged treat or something they knew she'd eat," I replied, "and then stuck the gum in her fur while she was asleep, so she wouldn't start barking and raise the alarm."

Around us, the crowd murmured in response. I looked around, having forgotten that others could be listening. "How awful," said a voice, and I turned to see Helen Bradley, the woman whom George had run into earlier, standing in the crowd. Her blue eyes were creased with concern. "Who would do such a dreadful thing—to a poor, innocent animal?"

Louise hobbled over to her friend and laid a hand on her shoulder. Angie looked up at her friend, sniffing. "I thought we had a chance at Best in Show this year," she whispered. "But now . . ." She shook her head sadly.

In response, Marshmallow Fluff got to her feet and woofed softly at Angie, placing a huge, fluffy paw on her leg. Angie looked down at the dog and rubbed the top of her head. "It's okay, Marshy. It's not your fault. We'll get through this."

Seeing that Marshmallow Fluff had recovered, most of the crowd began to disperse, with a couple of folks, including Helen and a young woman with blond hair in a pixie cut, hanging back to console Angie. Louise made her way over to a chair and slumped into it, her brow creased with contained rage. She saw me watching her, and when our eyes met, she inclined her head twice, calling me over. I crossed over to where she was, with George and Bess in tow. "This is bad news, Red," she said once we'd gotten within hearing range. "I've heard of this kind of thing happening at dog shows, and we're lucky Marshmallow made it out alive. She just as easily could have been poisoned, if some nutcase is looking to take out the competition. Now . . ." She gave me a serious look. "Are you still working as an amateur detective? Your father tells me you've managed to close a bunch of cases these past few years."

I chuckled. "Well," I said, "it isn't as if I go looking for problems to solve, but they just seem to find me."

George cut in. "She's being modest, Ms. Alain. When it comes to mysteries, there's no one better to have on your side than Nancy Drew. I can't tell you how many times Nancy has stopped criminals—even experienced ones—in their tracks. They don't take Nancy seriously, and it lands them in jail."

I blushed and nudged George with my elbow.

"What?" she replied. "It's true. If anyone could sniff around this dog show and figure out who drugged Marshmallow Fluff, it's you."

Louise's eyes lit up. "Yes! Will you do it, Red? If one dog is in danger, they all are. And if Angie manages to fix up Marshmallow's coat enough for her to compete, then the perpetrator might try again. We can't let that happen!" She grabbed my arm with her strong, freckled hand, her voice soft. "Please, honey. Do it for the puppies." She turned to look at Marge, who was sitting quietly beside her. Right on cue, the bull terrier cocked her head and gazed at me soulfully with her little black eyes.

I smiled. "How can I say no?"

"How indeed?" Louise crowed, all vestiges of tenderness gone. She rubbed her hands together, as if hungry for a fight. "Whoever tried to take down that pup is going to be sorry they ever crossed you, aren't they, Red? Detective Nancy Drew is on the case!"

The sound of Louise's clarion call made Helen, Angie, and all the other people around us stop talking and glance over curiously.

I waved at the onlookers, smiling awkwardly. "Nothing to worry about!" I called out. "Louise!" I whispered, bending to her ear. "I know you're excited, but if we're going to find the culprit, we'll have to keep a low profile. Do you get my drift?"

Louise's eyebrows rose, and her mouth formed an O. "Right, right," she whispered conspiratorially. "Any one of these people could have done it. We can't let them know we're onto them."

"Exactly," I agreed. "I'm fairly certain the perpetrator is also a competitor in the dog show—it's the only motive that makes any sense. Do you know most of the competitors pretty well, Louise?"

Louise scanned the crowd. "Sure do. There are only a few newcomers that I can see—and I doubt any one of them would do something like this. A newbie wouldn't have a chance at Best in Show, anyhow—so why bother with sabotage? No, it would have to be a real contender."

"That's a good point," I said. "And it helps narrow down our suspects."

"I've got an idea," Bess piped up. "Nancy, since you need to do the dog handler training with Louise before the show tomorrow and Sunday, she can introduce you to all the other competitors then. And George and I can go shopping for costumes for the masquerade ball tonight. How does that sound?"

I slapped myself in the forehead. "The ball! I'd completely forgotten!" The dog show had been scheduled for the same weekend as the winter carnival's annual masquerade ball, held in the grand ballroom of the Château Frontenac. All the dog show competitors were invited to attend. In fact, the winter carnival had named this year's party the Dog Ball in honor of the show.

"Well, I didn't forget for a moment!" Bess exclaimed.

"Shocker," George said with a smirk.

"Oh, please!" said Bess, elbowing her cousin in the ribs. "You know you're just as excited as I am! Masks! Live music! An all-you-can-eat buffet! Come on—admit it!"

George looked at Bess, biting her lip. Finally she blew out her cheeks in defeat. "Fine!" she said. "I'm excited. Thrilled, even! Are you happy now?"

"Yes!" Bess replied, throwing her hands up. "Now let's leave Nancy to do her thing—you trust us to pick out a costume for you, right, Nance?"

I looked back and forth between them—super-feminine Bess with her blush-pink sweater dress and cream-colored tights, and ultra-edgy George in her gray graphic tee, ripped jeans, and sneakers. I figured that between them, they'd probably find something that fell somewhere in the middle, which suited me just fine. "Surprise me," I said with a smile.

"Oh, we will," George replied, waggling her eyebrows.

After I waved goodbye to my friends, Louise and Marge led me into the main showroom. You'd think a room full of dogs would be loud and chaotic, but the scene before me was surprisingly orderly. Some handlers were practicing running their dogs around the ring and obeying commands, while others were on the sidelines at tables, trimming their dogs' nails, or blow-drying and brushing their coats until they shone. "It's like a full-service salon in here," I observed, and Louise nodded vigorously.

"Nothing but the best for these pups," she said. "If you want to win, every detail matters."

I walked by a woman in a cherry-red jumpsuit, who seemed to be posing for a selfie with her large standard poodle. The poodle's black coat was shorn close to its body, except for the signature booties around its feet and the poofs of fur on top of its head and at the tip of its tail. After tapping the shutter on her phone several times, the woman peered at the screen to scrutinize the results, her ruby-painted lips puckered in concentration. Louise noticed me looking at the woman and stopped before we passed. "Hey, V," Louise said. "Meet my new handler—Nancy Drew."

The woman called V looked up at me, her dark eyes a challenge. "Oho," she said. "You bringing in a ringer, old girl?"

Louise hooted. "No," she said. "Nancy's as green as grass—but clever like a fox. She learns fast. Don't you count Marge out yet, V. Just because I'm out of the running doesn't mean she is."

"Well then," V said. "Allow me to introduce myself to the competition." She turned to me and extended a manicured, bejeweled hand. "Valencia Vasquez, of Los Angeles. And this is my two-time champion, Miss Hollywood Garden." She gestured toward the poodle, who I now noticed wore a bejeweled collar to match her owner's rings.

"Charmed," I replied, shaking her hand. "Well, don't let us keep you. I'm sure you have a lot to do!"

V raised a sculpted eyebrow and tittered. "Not nearly as much as you do, my dear!" she said, and turned back to Hollywood Garden to pose for another selfie.

"Boy," I muttered to Louise as we turned away. "She's a real peach, isn't she?"

"If looks could kill, every dog show V's ever gone to would be a crime scene," Louise said airily. "But it's all part of the game. V has been on the show circuit for years now—she's a consummate professional. She's like her dog, really. That poodle looks like a gussied-up birdbrain, but in reality, she's one of the smartest, most athletic competitors in this room. It's something to keep in mind, Red. If you want to see the truth of a person, just look at their dog." I gazed over at Louise as she said this, with sturdy, loyal Marge at her side. I had to admit, owner and pet seemed to make a perfect pair. Maybe there was something to Louise's strange advice.

We stopped as we reached the ring, and Louise solemnly handed me Marge's lead. "Time to warm up with a few laps around," she said. "I'll hop along next to you as best I can and give you some tips." Louise gave me a small clicker and some treats to help correct Marge's gait as we went. "Now," she said as we began to move forward. "All the movement should come from your hips—brisk, smooth strides. Keep your upper body and the hand holding the leash still. Imagine you've got a glass of water on your head and you don't want it to spill. Let your other hand move naturally, as if you were out for a stroll in the park."

Suddenly what had seemed like nothing at all felt very, very complicated. I felt like a clumsy oaf at first, taking steps that were either too small or too large, almost getting myself tangled up in the lead. But after a little while, I felt a certain rhythm with Marge, and things got a little easier.

"Good!" Louise nodded, trying to keep up. "Now you're getting it, Red!"

She stopped to watch us run a couple of laps, and then we slowed down again so she could keep up with our pace and point out a few of the other competitors. There was a bespectacled man from West Texas named Curtis who was showing a Boston terrier; the pixie blonde from earlier, whose name was Alice—her shih tzu was apparently a pretty strong contender— and a handsome young man named Byung, who had traveled all the way from Korea to showcase his chow chow, named Golden Supernova. Finally we stopped for a water break, for both Marge and me. Louise went off to chat up one of the judges, just to make sure they'd changed Marge's handler from Louise's name to mine. A few moments after she'd left, Alice walked up to me. She held her brown-and-white shih tzu in her arms and was petting it nervously as she approached.

"Um, hello," she said, having a hard time looking me in the eye. "I, uh, hear you're Marge's new handler."

"Yes, I'm Nancy," I said brightly. "You're Alice?"

The woman nodded. "Yes, Alice Chesterfield."

"And who's this?" I asked, gesturing toward her dog.

"This is Piàoliang de Gōngzhǔ," Alice said seriously, as if she were introducing royalty. Her whole demeanor changed once we were talking about her dog.

"Wow," I said.

"It's Chinese for 'beautiful princess,'" Alice explained. "I call her Pia for short. Shih tzus are an ancient breed, you see, and Pia's bloodline goes back all the way to the seventeenth century, to a dog gifted to the emperor by the Dalai Lama." Pia, as if she understood that her noble lineage was being discussed, raised her head and looked at me imperiously.

"Wow," I repeated, unsure of what else to say.

"Um, anyway, Nancy," Alice continued, her shyness returning. "I wanted to talk to you, because I heard that you were looking into who put the gum in Marshmallow Fluff's fur."

"Yes . . . I suppose I am." I smiled politely, but I was pretty annoyed. If Alice already knew about my investigation, it was possible everyone did. So much for keeping a low profile!

"Well, normally I don't like to butt my head into things like this," Alice said. "But in New York we always say, 'If you see something, say something,' so . . ." She bit her lip.

I took a step closer to the woman. "Did you see someone do this to Ms. Wilson's dog, Alice?"

"I didn't see her do anything," Alice said quickly. "I'm not making any accusations. But . . . I did see Valencia Vasquez walking toward the crates a little while before it happened. And I've literally never seen her without a stick of gum in her mouth." Alice looked uncomfortable. "Again, I'm not saying she did it. Valencia is a good friend of mine. But if it was her . . . I just want to do the right thing. You know?"

I put my hand on Alice's arm. "Of course. Thank you for the information," I told her. "I'll look into it."

Alice smiled at me—a quick, anxious smile—before she put Pia over her shoulder and hurried away. As she retreated, the shih tzu regarded me with the kind of look a king gives a peasant begging in the street. *Boy,* I thought, *Helen Bradley was right. The people at these dog shows are certainly unique.*

I took a deep breath and sighed. I'd been in Quebec City for only a few hours, and already a tangled web of possible suspects was growing in this petty crime I was investigating. And something in my gut told me that this was only the beginning.

❦

CHAPTER THREE

Belle of the Dog Ball

AFTER A COUPLE OF HOURS OF HANDLER training, Louise and I made our way back to the Château Frontenac to relax before the evening's festivities. I climbed the magnificent golden spiral staircase up to the second floor to my room. We'd been in such a hurry earlier, when we dropped off our luggage, that I'd barely gotten a chance to check it out properly. But after an appreciative glance around the room—with its white paneled walls and big picture window overlooking the city—I collapsed onto the welcoming bed and fell asleep.

When I woke again later, the room was filled with

the rosy light of dusk, and someone was hammering on my door. Rubbing the sleep from my eyes, I plodded over to the door and opened it to find George and Bess standing there, dressed from head to toe for the masquerade ball. "Rise and shine, sleepyhead!" Bess said brightly. "It's time to party!"

All the drowsiness left me as soon as the sunshine that is Bess Marvin entered the room. She was dressed in a floor-length, icy blue gown with silver and blue sequins covering the bodice. Over her face she wore a silvery mask with many points coming off it, like a sparkling snowflake. "Bess, it's lovely!" I told her. "And so winter-appropriate!"

I turned to George, who was wearing a short violet dress with a skirt that flared out from the waist. Matching satin gloves covered her arms, and she wore a black-and-violet cat mask over her face, complete with pointed ears and wispy black whiskers. "You're wearing a cat mask to the Dog Ball?" I chuckled.

"What?" George said. "I like to be edgy. Anyway, what can I say? I'm a cat person."

"Maybe you're just hoping one of the guys will chase you," Bess teased.

George blushed and elbowed Bess in the ribs. "Hardly," she said. "Anyway, Nance—you're going to love what we picked out for you!" She stuffed a shopping bag into my arms and waved me into the bathroom to change.

Bess's face lit up when I emerged a few minutes later. "Oh!" she exclaimed. "Oh, it's even more perfect than I expected!" George gave me two thumbs-up.

"You two really know me well," I said, smiling shyly. The strapless burgundy dress was velvety soft and flowed in ripples to the floor—simple but elegant. My friends had picked out two gold cuffs for my wrists, and on my face I wore a brown-and-gold beaked mask, with striped feathers arching off the two corners like pyramid-shaped ears.

"An owl mask for our all-seeing bird of prey!" George quipped.

"Hunting down bad guys in America and beyond!" Bess added.

I laughed. I could always count on Bess and George to keep me from taking myself too seriously. "Well, ladies," I said. "The ballroom awaits!"

When we made our way back downstairs, the lobby was buzzing with guests, virtually all of them dressed to the nines for the big party. I noticed with amusement the large number of dog masks on display—often worn by the owner to match their pet. Winding through the crowd, we followed the signs to the Château Frontenac's majestic ballroom. Bess's jaw dropped, and George instantly began rummaging in her purse for her phone as soon as we got through the door. The room was vast and breathtakingly beautiful. Gigantic windows reached all the way up to the cathedral ceilings, and eight massive crystal chandeliers cast warm yellow light down onto the scene below. On a raised stage at the back of the room, a ten-piece band was already playing a classic waltz for guests on the dance floor. Waiters and waitresses walked around the room with delicious-smelling trays of appetizers and drinks. "*Bonsoir, mesdemoiselles,*" a young hostess said as we walked in. "*Bienvenue a la Soirée du Chien!*"

"*Merci beaucoup*," George said, bowing her head politely. She turned to Bess and me, her cat mask making her look even more mischievous than usual. "Well, I don't know about you girls, but I'm ready to eat! That poutine feels a world away."

"I want to explore a little bit first," Bess replied, lacing her arm through mine. "C'mon, Nancy, let's take in the sights!"

As we made our way around the room, I spied Valencia Vasquez, holding a champagne flute and chatting up a gentleman wearing a steel-gray wolf mask. She was wearing a silky black dress and an elegant canine mask that looked very much like Hollywood Garden. When she saw us coming, she waved the man away and turned to scrutinize our outfits. "Nancy, my dear," she crooned. "You clean up nice. And who's this pretty little thing?"

I gritted my teeth. "This is Bess Marvin. Bess, meet Valencia Vasquez. Her poodle is competing in the Non-Sporting Group."

"Nice to meet you," Bess said, nodding her head.

Considering Valencia's blunt honesty, I took a chance and asked, "So, V, you've been in the dog show game a while. What do you think of the competition this year?"

Valencia took a sip of her champagne and scanned the room. "Eh," she replied. "A lot of the same faces as usual—Helen is about as threatening as a can of peaches, but she's got a pretty solid game. The judges like her down-home, suburban charm. She did well in last year's shows in Chicago and Amsterdam—and actually took Best of Breed in Helsinki. Charles is hit-or-miss; he only shows on occasion. And as for Alice"—here Valencia scowled, as if she had tasted something bitter—"you never know what will happen with her around."

"Oh?" I asked. "She seemed like kind of the quiet type."

"A snake is quiet too," Valencia scoffed.

Bess and I exchanged a glance. I had told her about the conversation I had that afternoon with Alice, when she told me Valencia should be my number one suspect.

"And how about the others?" I asked, hoping to squeeze Valencia for as much gossip as possible while she had a belly full of champagne.

"That one"—she pointed to the large man who I'd seen in the crowd when we were trying to revive Marshmallow—"he's new. His name is Joe something, Joe Cook, I think. Now there's a quiet type if I've ever seen one. He's barely said a word to anyone since he arrived. Got a basset hound competing—Shirley Heartbreaker. Nice dog, but it will be his heart broken when he finds out that she hasn't a fighting chance."

I glanced over to look at Joe, who was pressed up against a wall on the far side of the room. He wore a plain scarlet mask over his face and kept checking his watch. "Doesn't look like he's having much fun," I commented.

Valencia *tsk*ed and picked up another glass of champagne from a passing waiter. "Why do a dog show if you're not going to enjoy it?" she asked.

Why indeed? I wondered.

"Louise is usually a pretty tough one to beat,"

Valencia went on, "but now that she's got you in as her handler, that makes Marge a little bit of a question mark." She looked straight at me, a challenge in her eyes.

"We'll see," I said, meeting her gaze.

Valencia smiled, her red lips stretching wide like the Cheshire cat. "Yes," she said. "We will."

After a little more exploring, we made our way to the buffet table, where George was standing with a plate piled high with delicacies. "So," she said through a mouthful of food. "Narrow down the list of suspects at all?"

I frowned. "I didn't narrow it down as much as make it longer. Alice already basically accused Valencia of the stunt. But I'm not totally convinced Valencia is the one we want, and according to her, Alice herself isn't quite what she seems, and neither is the new guy over there—Joe. It almost seems like anyone could have done it. Every one of them has a motive. They all want to win."

"How about Mr. Dubois over there?" George

asked, glancing at something behind us. "What is he up to, do you think?"

I turned to see Charles Dubois, a *Phantom of the Opera*-style white mask covering half his face, lurking behind one of the tables where a few guests had left their bags and other belongings. He was covertly sifting through the pockets of a suit jacket that hung on the back of a chair; then he searched inside a purse on the table before moving on, glancing around to make sure no one had witnessed the act. Luckily, I turned back around quickly and he didn't notice us watching.

Bess covered her mouth with her hand. "What could he be looking for?" she murmured.

I shook my head. "Not sure—maybe something to use for blackmail? That's another good way to get people to drop out of the competition. All I know for sure is, Mr. Dubois just jumped to the top of my list of suspects." I picked a mini quiche off George's plate and popped it into my mouth. After chewing thoughtfully, I said to Bess and George, "I'd better keep an eye on him. You two keep your eyes peeled for anyone else doing something suspicious. Someone in this room is hiding something, and I'm going to find out who."

As I walked past them, I almost ran into Helen Bradley, who was standing next to us, nibbling at a plate of baby carrots and celery. "Oops!" I said. "I've got to stop bumping into you like this!"

Helen laughed and waved away my apology. "Enjoying the party?" she asked, gesturing toward the crowd of masked guests. "I love a good masquerade. It's always fun pretending to be something you're not—it's like Halloween for grown-ups!"

I nodded. "It's fun," I agreed. "But I could never really get into pretend games. Too easy for me to see through the lie, I guess." I shrugged. "It's a blessing and a curse!"

Helen took a long sip of her drink. "You must not like reading mystery stories, then," she guessed.

I laughed. "Oh, I love mystery stories," I replied. "The problem is, I always figure it out by the second chapter."

Helen opened her mouth and looked like she was

about to respond when she seemed to feel something in her purse. She put her drink and plate down on a table nearby, pulled out her phone, and glanced at the screen. "If you'll excuse me," she said, pressing her phone to her chest, "I have to take this. It's my husband—whenever he's home alone with the kids, he calls me every hour!" She shook her head, chuckling and muttering, "Men!" before turning away and putting the phone up to her ear.

I began walking a slow circuit around the room, trying to watch the movements of all the competitors, searching for anything out of the ordinary. After a little while, I saw the same gentleman with the wolf mask walk up to Bess, bow, and take her hand in his. Bess smiled and blushed before allowing herself to be led out onto the dance floor. She laughed as he twirled and dipped her to the sound of the music, which had changed to be more upbeat now that the night had progressed. She caught my eye in the crowd as I watched and waved to me, beaming. I waved back, shaking my head. Bess was like a flame in a world full of moths—drawing everyone close with her radiance.

After about half an hour of watching with no more information to speak of, I finally headed back to the buffet for a dinner break. I had just taken my fifth bite of chicken marsala when George ran up to the table where I was sitting, her eyes wide with barely concealed panic. I set the plate down and got up to meet her. "George, what's wrong?" I asked.

"It's Bess," George said, her voice choked with emotion. "I don't know where she is! I've been looking for her everywhere for the past ten minutes—I even checked her room—but I can't find her! She's not answering her phone. . . . She wouldn't have just left, Nancy!"

I gripped George's shoulder. It was so unusual to see her frantic like this that it threatened to infect me with panic too. "Okay," I said, as smoothly as I could. "Calm down, we'll find her. Let's ask around and see if anyone saw her leave."

Ten minutes later, we were no further along with

our search except for one other fact. The last person who we'd seen Bess with—the man with the wolf mask—was gone too. A heavy stone settled in my stomach. "The front desk," I said. "Maybe they saw something. We have to try."

George and I ran from the ballroom, still loud and crowded with partygoers, back into the empty lobby. The same concierge who'd been there when we arrived was standing behind the desk. "Excuse me," I asked him in a rush. "My name is Nancy Drew. We can't seem to find our friend. Her name is Bess Marvin—she's the blond-haired girl we checked in with this morning."

The concierge nodded. "I remember her. I don't recall seeing her leave from the front here, however. . . ." He turned to the computer and typed something in. His eyebrows went up. "Ah yes, I thought so. There was a message left for you, Miss Drew. Just about twenty minutes ago." He pulled an envelope from under the desk with my name printed on it in nondescript block letters. I tore it open and pulled out a single sheet of paper with the same block lettering written on it. George and I read it together.

> *Nancy Drew: We have taken your friend. If you want to see her again, drop your investigation immediately. Act normal, tell no one, and do not involve the police. If you do as we say, Bess will be returned to you as soon as the dog show is over. You don't want to find out what will happen if you ignore our orders. You have no idea who you're dealing with. Do the show and go home—or else.*

I turned to George, all the blood draining from my face.

"What are we going to do?" George whispered.

My pulse was roaring in my ears as I tried to understand how a little prank at a dog show had come to this. "I don't know," I said, feeling helpless and confused. "I don't know."

~

CHAPTER FOUR

A Wolf in the Night

"HI! YOU HAVE REACHED THE VOICE MAIL of Bess Marvin. I can't get to the phone right now, but if you leave a message, I'll get back to you as soon—"

I clicked my phone off and tried to breathe through the nausea rising into my throat. "Her phone is turned off—it's going straight to voice mail," I murmured to George. She blinked, dashing a tear from her face.

You're no good to Bess if you panic, I thought. *Focus. Think. Plan. What's your next move?*

"Can you interview the waitstaff?" I asked George, holding her shoulder to steady her. "Ask if any of them spoke to the man in the wolf mask—if they know anything about him at all."

George nodded, looking relieved to be given instructions. "What are you going to do?" she asked.

"Look for clues to where he might have taken her," I said. "If these people think we're going to just follow their orders and wait for them to bring her back, they're dead wrong." I felt my pulse slow and my back straighten as my fear transformed into a single-minded purpose. This town was full of obedient creatures at the moment—but I wasn't one of them.

George's mouth was pressed into a hard line. "Right," she said. But after a moment, her brow creased. "I just don't get it, though, Nancy. Why would someone resort to kidnapping, just over some kind of petty sabotage at a dog show? It doesn't make sense!"

"You're right, it doesn't," I agreed. "Which makes me think this must be about something else."

"Something else?" George asked. "Like what?"

"I don't know," I confessed. "But maybe when we started sniffing around about the attack on

Marshmallow Fluff, we stumbled into something bigger. Something these people don't want to risk me exposing." I shrugged. "I don't know," I repeated. "But that's my best guess until we get more information. I'm going to scour this place while Bess's trail is still warm and see what I can find."

"Okay," George said. "Text me if you find anything, and we'll meet up later." As I turned to go, she grabbed my arm and said, "Be careful, okay, Nance?"

I nodded, and we parted ways. I quickly ran up to my room to grab a coat, and then made my way outside. The hotel was shaped kind of like an empty square, with several enclosed parking lots in the middle, accessed through tunnels that ran through the belly of the building. Someone with a getaway car parked in one of these dark tunnels could have easily taken Bess out a side door and into the car quickly and without being seen. I tried the one closest to the ballroom first. A bellhop was standing near the door, bouncing up and down on his heels for warmth.

"Good evening, mademoiselle," he said as I

approached, his breath cascading out in rolling clouds. "Can I help you with anything?"

"Actually yes," I said. "I'm looking for my friend—she's blonde, and she was wearing a light-blue dress and a silver mask tonight. Last I saw her, she was with a man in a dark suit and a wolf mask. Did you happen to see them leave?"

The bellhop cocked his head and reached into the pocket of his coat. "A silver mask—like this?" His outstretched hand held Bess's mask.

I reached out and grabbed it; just holding it in my hands made me feel like Bess was somehow within reach. "Yes, this is hers—where did you find it?"

"I went inside to get a coffee about forty-five minutes ago," the bellhop said. "I was only gone for maybe ten minutes, but when I got back, I found this mask on the ground over there." He pointed to a parking space just outside the nearest tunnel.

I ran over to where he'd pointed and noticed some tire tracks imprinted in the snow. There were some strange, grayish-white fibers stuck into the tracks—could they hold a clue to where Bess might have been taken? I pulled a handkerchief from my purse and gathered some of the fibers into it so I could look at them more closely later.

I stood, planning to return to the bellhop to ask him more questions, when a blur of movement from the opposite tunnel caught my eye. A tall figure in a black parka, the hood pulled low over his face, was watching me, and I wondered why. "Excuse me," I called out to him.

The figure turned around and began to walk away, through the tunnel toward the street. "Wait!" I yelled. But that only seemed to propel him faster, and within moments, I'd lost sight of him.

"Oh, no you don't," I muttered to myself, and took off running. Thank goodness I was wearing flats, I thought as I charged across the parking lot and through the dark tunnel. I popped out onto a busy thoroughfare lit by streetlights and scanned the street for the figure. He was about thirty feet away, heading toward town at a brisk clip. I chased after him, shouldering past groups of tourists, the frigid air burning my lungs. He must have heard the rapid *slap slap slap* of my shoes on the pavement coming closer, because he turned to see me approaching and immediately took a sharp right to cross the street at the red light. I pushed myself for a burst of speed, managing to make it halfway across the road before the light began to change.

But there must have been a slick of black ice right near the curb, because before I knew what was happening, my feet had gone out from under me, and I fell headfirst into the pavement. I managed to put my hands up before my face hit the ground, but I couldn't save my knees from whacking painfully against the asphalt. I looked up to find the figure, but my eyes were blinded by headlights—coming right toward me.

I gasped and tried to get up, only to slip and fall again. The car was virtually on top of me now and didn't look like it was going to stop. Time seemed to slow as the yellow light filled my whole vision, my whole world.

Suddenly I felt a firm grip on my coat, and the

sensation of being yanked off the street with extreme force. My hip bumped the curb as I slid away, and I watched in horrified silence as a black taxicab ran straight over the spot where I'd been lying just seconds ago. I scrambled to my feet and hissed with pain, feeling the spot on my side where I was sure a bruise was forming.

"You're welcome," said a voice next to me, and I turned to see the tall figure I'd been chasing standing there. Had I heard that voice before somewhere?

I felt my face get hot with anger. "You never would have needed to do that if you hadn't run away in the first place. Who are you? Why don't you want to talk to me?"

There was a pause. "You're not going to let this go, are you?" the man finally asked.

I shook my head. "Whatever it is that's going on here—you better believe I'm not letting it go. My friend is in danger."

The man's brows furrowed at this bit of news. "Your friend . . . ?" he asked.

"Bess Marvin. She's been kidnapped," I told him. "Whoever took her left a note with the front desk threatening to hurt her if I don't stop snooping around. Do you know anything about that?"

The man cursed under his breath and muttered, "It's even worse than I thought." Sighing, he said, "Well, you give me no choice then." He stuck his hand into his parka and began to pull something out.

My heart leaped into my throat. Was he reaching for a gun? A knife?

I relaxed as I saw what he was really going for—a badge. It had a picture of the globe with a sword running through it, and the words INTERNATIONAL POLICE— INTERPOL engraved above and below. On the ID card above was a photo of a familiar face.

"Charles Dubois?" I said incredulously.

Charles pulled the hood of his parka down, revealing an expression full of frustration. "You're an undercover agent?" I asked.

"*Oui*, for now," he said. "Though you aren't making it easy for me, mademoiselle!"

"You aren't here because someone is sabotaging the dog show," I said, my mind whirling. "You're here because of something else, aren't you?"

Charles cleared his throat and studied the street around us. "Walk with me," he murmured. "If we are going to talk about this, we need to do it on the move."

We began strolling side by side, heading back in the direction of the château. "For several years now," Charles began, "I have been investigating an international jewel thief who is allegedly traveling around the world, posing as a dog show exhibitor. We got wind of the situation from some of our agents in Europe—but the problem was that no one knew anything about the thief, nothing at all."

I was confused. "Why would a jewel smuggler want to pretend to be a dog show competitor?"

"When you travel with animals, particularly show dogs," Charles explained, "it's easy to sneak things through customs in the crates. Show dogs are given a bit of leeway because their owners are so . . ." Charles seemed to have difficulty with what he wanted the next word to be. "Particular," he finally said, "about their animals. And no one would blink at an exhibitor with several championships under their belt doing a lot of international travel. It's part of the job, after all, going from one show to another."

I nodded. "Okay, that makes sense."

Charles went on. "The only information we have is snippets of recorded conversations picked up about someone called 'Surefire.' We figure that's the thief's code name, so we've been able to trace this person from one dog show to another, but we've never been able to catch him or her in the act. I've been posing as an exhibitor myself, competing in show after show, in an effort to arrest Surefire. Before this I was in Finland, and then the latest bread crumb led us here, to my hometown, so I've been very hopeful that I'll be able to track the thief down in Quebec City. But then this whole chewing-gum debacle happened . . . and you showed up. *La petite inspecteur.*"

I cringed a little at the word "*petite*," which sounded insulting coming out of his mouth. "Hey!" I said, stopping in the middle of the sidewalk. "Louise Alain asked for my help, and I gave it. If I had known what I was walking into, I would never have put my friend at risk."

Charles stopped too and rubbed his face with his hands. "Oh, I know, mademoiselle. *Je suis désolé.* The thing is, I've been chasing this criminal for a long time—I don't want him to fall through my fingers. And with this newest development with Mademoiselle Marvin, it's all become very . . . complicated."

"Maybe," I said. "But it's not just complicated for us—it's complicated for them, too. Kidnapping Bess was a risky move. A desperate move. Now we know for certain that they're here, and unless they were very careful, they will have left behind a clue." I reached into my purse and pulled out the handkerchief with the fibers inside. "And let me tell you something," I added, handing the evidence to Charles. "They weren't very careful."

Charles touched the fibers with his finger and smiled. "Well, Mademoiselle Drew," he said. "Perhaps

having you around won't be such a headache, after all."
He began to pick up the pace again, taking a shortcut
back toward the hotel. *"Dépêchez-vous!"* he said, hurrying me along. "The clock is ticking, and you and I have
a crime to solve."

CHAPTER FIVE

On the Scent

AS WE MADE OUR WAY BACK TO CHÂTEAU Frontenac, moments after I'd texted George to meet us in the lobby, I spied Louise and Angie walking out the front door, with Marge and Marshmallow Fluff in tow. Angie was holding both leashes so Louise could concentrate on walking with her crutch.

"Aha," said Louise as we approached, eyeing us both suspiciously. "Are you consorting with the enemy now, Nancy—or just grilling him for information?"

Charles coughed and gave me a warning look.

"I was just getting a little overheated inside that

crowded ballroom," I lied, "so he brought me out here for some fresh air."

"How kind of you, Chuck," Louise said, still suspicious. Charles cringed visibly at the nickname. "But don't think you can charm your way to Best in Show!" She waggled her finger at him disdainfully before turning to me again. "Where are your two girlfriends, anyway? Why didn't they help you?"

Charles coughed again, more forcefully this time.

Louise stared at him. "What's with you?" she asked. "Cold getting to you?"

"Uh, the girls turned in early for the night," I said quickly. I felt terrible for lying to Louise, but I had no choice. "It's been a long day for all of us." I turned to the dogs, hoping to change the subject. "Oh, Marshmallow—you look well after your ordeal!" Sure enough, the big white dog seemed no worse for wear, except for some small tufts of hair missing from a couple of spots on her back. Her huge pink tongue lolled out in excitement at the sound of her name, and she happily slurped my hand, covering it entirely with goo.

"Yech," I said with a strained smile as I wiped it on my coat. "Good girl. Nice girl."

"I did my best with her coat," Angie said with a shrug. "The gum wasn't that badly stuck, so I got most of it off without having to cut the fur. Hopefully it won't hurt her chances with the judges too much."

"It's hardly noticeable," I assured her, scratching the big sheepdog behind the ears. "She's a great dog, They'd be fools not to see that."

Angie beamed, and the dogs began to pull impatiently on their leads. "Duty calls!" Angie called out, and the two women walked past us down the sidewalk.

"Whew," I said to Charles when they were finally gone, letting out a breath I didn't know I was holding. "I hate not being able to tell her what's really going on."

"It's the only way to keep everyone safe—and find your friend," Charles assured me. "Keep the circle small. Louise Alain keeps secrets like a sieve holds water—she's the last person who needs to know all this." He held open the door and I walked inside.

I smirked. "You just don't like that she calls you Chuck."

"Pah!" Charles spat. "'Chuck' is what you call a call a piece of meat—and not a very good one, mind you." Clearly, I had hit a nerve.

"Fine," I agreed. "We won't tell Louise. But not telling George is a deal breaker. She and I come as a pair."

Charles sighed hugely and pinched the bridge of his long nose with his manicured fingers. "All right, all right! You can tell her. Ach . . . one little girl detective is bad enough, and now I have to deal with two. . . ."

I crossed my arms and gave him a stern look. "Without this 'little girl,' Monsieur Dubois, you would have no leads at all!"

Charles raised his hands in mock surrender. "*Alors*, you are correct, mademoiselle. Let's find Mademoiselle George and get upstairs quickly so I can contact my superiors."

George appeared from a hallway just as Charles and I walked into the crowded lobby. Apparently the masquerade ball had just ended, and guests were still milling about before heading up to their rooms for the night. "George!" I called out over the murmur of conversations. She heard me and hurried over, casting a questioning look at Charles standing beside me. "Um, I'll explain in the elevator," I murmured, casting glances around at who might be listening.

George nodded wordlessly and followed Charles and me into the closest elevator, where two other guests were standing. Charles pushed the button for the penthouse. Just as the doors were about to close, Valencia Vasquez glided into the elevator. "Ah!" she sighed with relief. "Just made it." She yawned luxuriously, and in the waft of her breath came the distinct scent of cherries. I wrinkled my nose—not my favorite smell. "So," she said, eyeing me, "did you enjoy the party, Nancy?"

"It certainly was something," I said truthfully.

"I saw your friend nabbed the handsome wolf man as her dance partner. I have to admit, I'm a little jealous," she told us.

I felt my breath catch in my throat and Charles

stiffen beside me. "Who is he, anyway?" I asked carefully. "Have you seen him before—one of the dog owners, maybe?"

V shook her head. "No, I'd remember him if I had. And anyway, I overheard him telling her that he doesn't even like dogs, so I can't imagine why he'd want to hang out with the likes of us!" She laughed. "Well," she said as the elevator doors opened. "This is me! Good night, all!"

It wasn't until the final guest had departed and the elevator doors were shut that Charles stabbed the emergency stop button. The car lurched to a halt in between floors, and George nearly jumped out of her skin.

"Hey!" she exclaimed. "What are you doing? Nancy, should I punch this guy or what?"

"No, no!" I stammered. "He's okay—Charles is with the international police! He's undercover."

"Oh," George said, sagging with relief. And then a moment later, "Oh!" She perked up again, realizing the elevator was less dangerous and the situation more interesting than she'd expected. She waggled her eyebrows. "A secret agent! Wait . . . so you must have been right, Nancy—this is about more than just some chewing gum, isn't it?"

I nodded. "A lot more." While I filled George in, Charles took a photograph with his phone of the grayish-white fibers I'd found in the tire tracks and sent it to his bosses at Interpol. By the time I had finished my story, Charles's phone had already binged an answer.

"Paper fibers," he said, looking up at us, "probably from a pulping factory. That's their best guess without actually seeing the evidence firsthand. It's a good guess—there are quite a few such factories in the city, and some of them are abandoned. We've seen them used before as hideouts. . . ." Charles tapped his chin, looking like he was piecing it all together. "At this time of year they would need to turn on the power for heat. Which would require going to the factory before picking her up . . ."

"Okay—let's go! What are we waiting for?" George said, moving to restart the elevator.

Charles turned to her, clearly shaken out of his thoughtful reverie. He put his hand on George's arm. "Mademoiselle," he said, "it is not that easy. We can't just go running to every factory in town looking for your friend. These fibers might not have anything to do with the kidnapping, even. Let the professionals do their work. I promise you, I will keep you and Nancy updated."

George opened her mouth to argue, but I shook my head. George swallowed the words and stood silent, her face a thundercloud.

"*Merci,*" Charles said. "For now, let us go back to our rooms. It's late, and tomorrow is a big day . . . for more reasons than one. No matter what, you two need to act as if everything is normal. Your friend Bess has taken ill, or gone on an errand—something to explain her absence. If the enemy catches wind of my identity, or that you two are still actively trying to root him out, I cannot guarantee the safety of Mademoiselle Marvin."

I gritted my teeth. Doing nothing was never my

strong suit. But there was no other way right now. I nodded.

"*Bien,*" Charles said approvingly. "The show must go on." He then restarted the elevator and pushed the button for the ninth floor, where most of the dog show competitors were staying. "Ach!" Charles exclaimed as the elevator lurched into life once again. "In all the excitement, I've forgotten all about young Coco. She'll need walking, and here I am with all this work to do."

"We'd be happy to walk her for you," I offered. "I need the practice . . . and frankly, I can't imagine getting much sleep tonight, with things as they are."

Charles looked at the two of us skeptically, but finally relented. "*D'accord.* But please, whatever you do, don't allow her to consort with neighborhood mongrels or eat any rubbish from the ground! That's the last thing I need. First a kidnapping, then a dog with a tummy ache on show day . . ."

Ten minutes later, after a lengthy speech about Coco's very particular care, George and I were back on the street, walking Coco the Weimaraner around the perimeter of the hotel. "I don't know what Charles was talking about," George commented. "I think this dog would rather starve to death than eat anything other than gourmet cuisine."

I chuckled. Like her owner, Coco Diamonds Are Forever was used to the finer things in life. She walked with her elegant gray head held high, looking down on any other dogs that came by and barked or tried to sniff her. Louise certainly seemed to be onto something with the idea that dogs mirrored their owners.

"Hey," George said quietly as we turned a corner. "Isn't that Joe? That big guy from the dog show?"

I looked where she was pointing and saw a hulk of a man across the street from us, wearing a brown parka and walking a basset hound, who herself was dressed in a fleece overcoat and boots. "I think so," I replied, squinting to see better in the dark.

As we watched, another man jogged to catch up with him. He said something to Joe, but instead of stopping to talk to him, Joe waved the man away and began to walk faster. However, this didn't seem to deter the man, who pursued Joe down the street.

"Let's cross here," I muttered to George, who nodded knowingly. I wanted to see exactly how this was going to play out.

Pulling our own parkas down over our faces, we followed a little ways back as the man tried to keep pace with Joe's enormous strides away from him down a deserted side street. "Wait up," the man called out. "Bull's-Eye!"

At that, Joe stopped in the middle of the sidewalk and allowed the man to catch up with him. George and I dove behind a Dumpster to avoid being seen as Joe whirled around and grabbed the man by his coat collar, lifting him up from the ground like he weighed nothing.

The man yelped in shock. "Hey!" he protested, squirming in Joe's grip. "Let me go!"

Joe's voice was low and dangerous. "Listen very closely," he said. "You don't know me. Do you understand? You've never seen me before."

"Uh, okay," the man said, his voice full of fear. "Okay, man, be cool. I didn't mean any harm. Please."

Joe dropped the man, and he stumbled as he landed back on his feet. "You best remember that," he said. He took a wallet from his pants pocket and pulled a few bills from it. "Here," he said, handing the money to the man. "This never happened. Clear?"

"Y-yeah," the man stammered, stuffing the cash into his pocket. "Crystal."

The basset hound growled as the man backed away.

"It's okay, Shirley," Joe said, patting her on the head. "Let him go."

The man ran past us without noticing, intent on getting as far away as possible. Taking a page from his book, George and I snuck away while Joe was still focused on his dog.

Once we'd put a block of pavement between Joe and us, George and I brought Coco into a late-night café to catch our breath and warm up from the cold. "What was that about, do you think?" George asked.

I bit my lip. "Joe's hiding something, that much

is clear. We should keep a close eye on him—if he's involved in this, he might be able to lead us to Bess."

Bess.

Saying her name gave both of us pause. *Where is she right now?* I wondered. *Is she hurt? Is she scared?*

Back at the hotel, we returned Coco to Charles, and I invited George to stay with me in my room overnight. I didn't want to be alone, and I could tell she didn't want to be either. We both changed into pajamas and climbed into the big queen-size bed. We could almost pretend it was just another normal sleepover. After a while, I heard George's breathing grow regular as exhaustion finally overtook her worried mind.

Me, I watched the minutes pass on the bedside clock, each one feeling like an eternity.

Bess.

I sent a message out into the world, imagining that she could hear me, wherever she was.

I'll find you. Just hang on.

Somehow, at some point, I fell asleep.

CHAPTER SIX

The Show
Must Go On

BY THE TIME THE FIRST RAYS OF MORNING light were streaming through my hotel room window, I was already awake and showered, laying out several wardrobe options for the big show. Louise had said to wear something solid colored—pleasant to look at, but not distracting. After all, the judges were there to see Marge, not me. I was standing in my bathrobe, trying to choose between two outfits, when there was a knock at the door.

"It's me!" George's voice called out from the hallway. She'd left a little while ago to collect some breakfast from the buffet downstairs. I opened the door to find her standing with a tray full of goodies— pastries, fresh fruit, cheese, juice, and coffee. She was dressed in her usual uniform of jeans, high-tops, and her favorite gray hoodie.

"Oh, fantastic," I said, my mouth watering at the sight of it all. I moved out of the way so she could put it down on the table in the middle of my hotel room. I grabbed a slice of cheese and munched on it while I continued to stare at the clothes on my bed. "Can you help me decide what to wear?" I asked George. "I'm having an impossible time. I'm so distracted." I didn't have to say what I was distracted by—concentrating on what to wear to a dog show while Bess was being held hostage somewhere seemed completely crazy. But Charles said we had to keep behaving as if everything were normal, so we wouldn't tip off the kidnappers. They were probably watching our every move.

"Mmm, I'd go with the sage-green top and the brown slacks," George said, before taking a bite of a cherry turnover.

I picked up the soft green blouse and held it up against my chest. "Yeah, that's what I was leaning toward too, I just wasn't sure. Normally, I'd just ask—" I stopped in midsentence, and the name "Bess" hung in the air between us.

George closed her eyes and sighed. "We'll find her," she finally whispered. "Today."

I nodded, hope and self-doubt warring in my heart. "Today."

After I got dressed and we finished eating, George and I headed downstairs to find Louise, who we were accompanying to the convention center. The lobby was crowded with competitors—many of them loaded down with bags and equipment for the main event— and their dogs. We found Louise near the front desk, Marge standing guard at her side. Louise was wearing a black sweatshirt with a logo of a bull terrier wearing sunglasses and the words BULLY LIFE printed on it in big block letters.

"Well, good morning, girls!" Louise said merrily. "You ready for war?"

I gave her a small, nervous smile and shrugged. "As ready as I'll ever be," I said. "I'll do my best for you and Marge!"

Louise gave me a playful punch in the shoulder. "Of course you will, Red! Nothing to worry about." Suddenly she looked confused and scanned the room. "Hey, where's Blondie? I haven't seen her since the party last night."

I gritted my teeth and quickly thought up another lie. "She . . . I think Bess ate something that disagreed with her last night. She's still in her room with an upset stomach. I'm sure she'll be fine, though. Just needs some rest."

Louise sighed. "Ah—too bad. She's going to miss the big show!" She looked at her watch and gave a start. "Speaking of which, we're going to miss it too if we don't hurry. There should be a taxi waiting for us."

We followed her outside, where a large black car waited with its engine running. Nearby, I saw Charles and Coco about to get into an identical car in front of us. Before he climbed in, Charles caught my eye and dragged two fingers across his mouth in a zipping motion. I nodded and repeated the motion back. The secret was safe with me.

The next hour was a blur. We arrived at the convention center, which was full of exhibitors, dogs, and guests who'd come to watch the show from the stands. Louise and I checked in with Marge. Then we met up with George and proceeded to the large prep area where all the dogs and handlers stayed until their turn to show. The heat in the room was stifling—what with all the people and animals packed in, not to mention the dozens of hair dryers running as owners styled their dogs for the big moment. We were directed to an area with all the other entrants in the Terrier Group. Once we got Marge comfortably settled, Louise leaned over to give me an insider's view of the competition. "So," she began, "as you can see, the Terrier Group is dominated by a lot of cute, fuzzy types. You've got the Westie and the Scottie over there"—she pointed to a small white dog panting adorably next to a regal-looking black Scottish terrier—"and they're crowd favorites. We also have to watch out for the Jack Russell—judges like spunk—and the Kerry blue." She directed my attention to a smoke-gray dog with a distinctive snout and fur that covered its eyes.

"What an interesting-looking dog," I commented. "I've never seen one like that before."

Louise harrumphed. "Yes, well—Lady Grey is already a breed champion from other competitions. Great coat and color—and she shows very well in the ring. She's going to be a tough one to beat." At this, Marge looked up at Louise with her tiny black eyes and whined. "Oh, don't get your tail in a knot, Marge," Louise said, affectionately nudging the dog on the chin. "I still believe in you." She picked a microscopic speck of grit from Marge's coat and gave the dog a pat. "Marge is the best bully I've ever had—ideal head shape, nice glossy coat, and a good, strong body. And you've run with her in the ring. She's a dream."

I nodded. Even a total newbie like me could recognize a real showgirl when I saw one. Marge barely blinked an eye at having me as her new handler. She ran around that ring like she was born for it.

"If it's spunk they want," George broke in, scratching the dog behind her ears, "Marge has got it." Marge opened her mouth in a big, almost comedic doggie smile and turned to lap George's hand with a sloppy pink tongue.

"I'll give it my all, Louise, I promise," I said.

"I know you will, Red," Louise replied. "I know."

In a few minutes, a voice came over the PA system. "Attention, guests. Please find your seats—the competition is about to begin!"

The first to show was the Toy Group. Half a dozen tiny little dogs were trotted around the ring, one at a time, and then placed on a table to be examined by the judges. After all that was done, the three judges collected the points awarded to each breed, and a group winner was announced. Alice's shih tzu was the winner, much to the delight of the audience, and she punched the air with a victorious gesture before heading back to the holding area. She walked over to the water cooler, filled two cups, and brought one of them to Angie, who was sitting nervously on the sidelines, waiting for her turn.

A moment later Helen Bradley walked up to where we were standing, craning her neck to get a view of the competitors in the ring. "Oh, hello, Nancy!" she said with a smile. She was wearing a peach-colored blouse with a string of pearls and cream slacks.

"Hi, Helen," I said. "How's it going? Everything all right?"

Helen cocked her head. "Well, sure! Why wouldn't it be?" she asked.

I shrugged. "Well, the person who drugged Marshmallow is still at large—they could attack one of the competitors again."

"Goodness me, I hadn't thought of that," Helen said. "I heard you were looking into the matter—any ideas on who might have done it?"

I shook my head, again wishing that we'd been more successful in keeping that information to ourselves. If Helen knew, probably everyone did. "Nothing yet," I replied, and then turned my attention to her dog. "So, this is the famous Daisy!" The Doberman pinscher had two distinctive tan spots above her eyes that made her look like she was always surprised. She wore a beautiful rolled leather collar in a shade of blue that matched her owner's eyes. I reached out to pet her. The dog didn't flinch, but I could hear a quiet growl rise from her throat. I pulled my hand back.

"Daisy Rocket Ship Bradley!" Helen said in a stern, motherly voice. "Mind your manners!" She rolled her eyes and sighed. "I'm so sorry. You can pet her. She just gets so anxious on show days."

I nodded and reached my hand out again. This time Daisy bumped her head against my hand and closed her eyes. "Oh, I understand, I'm nervous too," I said, scratching behind her ears. "What a pretty collar," I added. "I've never seen one quite like it!"

"Thank you!" Helen beamed. "I make them myself. I have an online store, if you're interested. The Bradley Boutique. I sell handmade collars, dog tags, and other canine accessories. It works with my schedule—brings in a little extra cash, you know." She looked behind me. "Where's your friend, the blond girl?" she asked. "I've been wanting to ask her about that necklace she was wearing yesterday—I think she and I have similar taste in fashion!"

"She's not feeling well," I replied, the lie coming more easily now. "She decided to stay in her hotel room for the day."

Helen sucked her teeth and looked crestfallen. "Oh no! The poor thing," she said. "Awful that she has to miss the show. Well, I hope she feels better soon— oops! I think we're on! Break a leg, Nancy—I'll be watching you!"

I decided to take a bathroom break while I could, and by the time I returned, the Hound Group was lining up while the announcer called them in one by one. Joe Cook was standing at the end of the line with his basset hound, his foot tapping nervously on the linoleum. The Terrier Group was second to last to show, so I had some time to kill—and questioning Joe was a top priority after witnessing his suspicious behavior on the street last night. Taking the opportunity, I made my way toward him. When I was only a few feet away, I pretended to slip on the floor. "Aah!" I said, throwing my hands up. For such a big guy, Joe moved like lightning. He whirled around, and his arm shot out to catch me before I could fall. I feigned a look of grateful relief and said, "Thank you! Ugh—I'm so clumsy. It's my first time being a handler, and I'm a nervous wreck. How about you? Is this your first time too?"

Joe's smile didn't reach his eyes. "Uh, no. I've done a couple before," he said.

"Really!" I said. "Anywhere fun and exotic? I hear some of the other competitors have taken their dogs to international shows."

"I've been around," Joe replied vaguely. "Look, I'm sorry, miss, but I really need to concentrate—I'm about to go on."

"Of course!" I said, starting to back away. "Good luck, er . . . what's her name?" I asked, gesturing to Joe's dog.

"Shirley Heartbreaker," Joe answered. Hearing

her name, the basset hound looked up at him with her soft, sad eyes.

"Good name," I said. "Very fitting."

Joe nodded absently and glanced back toward the ring's entrance, where most of the other hounds had already been called. He wiped a bead of perspiration from his temple and muttered, "Gotta go!" before hurrying forward. I watched as he paused at the edge of the ring until the announcer called them out. As if he was shedding a skin, Joe's shyness evaporated as soon as he went under the lights, and he greeted the crowd with a wide smile. He proceeded to jog around the ring, amazingly light on his feet for a guy who was easily six foot three and three hundred pounds. I thought back to how he had lifted that guy off the ground in the alleyway like it was nothing. What was it that he'd called Joe?

Bull's-Eye.

It occurred to me that the names "Bull's-Eye" and "Surefire" meant kind of the same thing. Could there be a connection?

I was still musing on the possibility when Shirley Heartbreaker won the Best in Group for the hounds a few minutes later. Joe lifted up the dog and gave her a big kiss, to the delight of the crowd, before leaving the ring. It was only when the announcer belted out, "And now—the Terrier Group!" that I was jolted back to reality.

George was at my side in an instant, positively buzzing with excitement. "You're up! Go get 'em, tiger!"

I gave George a small smile and balled my hands into fists as my stomach did a few uncomfortable somersaults. I had been so caught up with everything else that was happening, I'd forgotten how much I hated being in front of an audience. Give me a good crime to solve, but please don't make me stand up in front of a bunch of people and do things. Like talk. Or dance. Or—God forbid—sing.

Seeing the look on my face, George gave me a quick hug and said, "It'll be okay."

"The dog show?" I asked. "Or . . ." My voice trailed off.

"Both," George said firmly.

I took a deep breath, willing my stomach to stop its gymnastics. "You're right," I replied. "I'm ready." I walked over to Louise and took Marge's lead from her hand.

Louise slapped me on the back. "You got this," she said cheerily.

I got in line behind the Kerry blue and her handler, an older woman in a conservative blue skirt suit, her gray hair cut into a neat bob. She eyed me and Marge critically, particularly when Marge sniffed her dog's rear end. "You're Louise's replacement, hmm?" she asked.

"Yes, ma'am," I replied.

"How nice," she said in a way that felt like she didn't mean it. "You know what they call those dogs, don't you?"

I shook my head.

"Clowns in dog suits," she said with a chuckle. "People don't really take them seriously." A minute later the announcer called her into the ring, and she dashed away, her dog following elegantly at her side.

I glowered after her. I hadn't felt competitive before—but I did now. "C'mon, Marge," I muttered down to her. "Let's show that lady how it's done."

Marge looked up at me with her big, goofy grin and licked my hand. And then the announcer was speaking again and saying, "Please welcome to the ring: our bull terrier, Marge—and her handler, Miss Nancy Drew!"

Just like Louise had shown me, I ran out onto the floor, keeping Marge close and putting on my most charming smile. We stopped for a moment to greet the judges and the crowd before making the long circuit around the ring. Despite my heart hammering in my ears, I concentrated on keeping an even pace and making my movements smooth. For her part, Marge ran perfectly by my side. Her little eyes sparkled under the lights, and she virtually capered around the track. It was clear how much she loved this—and the judges seemed to see it too. When we were done with the circuit, I brought Marge over to the judges' area, where one of them examined her from head to tail. Marge stood proudly at attention while the judge looked her over. When that was done, Marge and I lined up with the other terriers to await the judges' decision. I breathed a sigh of relief once we reached our spot—the hard part was over.

While the judges tallied up the points for each dog in the group, I absentmindedly scanned the crowd, blinking as dozens of cameras flashed in our direction. Then my eyes focused on something strange high up in the stands. A dark, contorted face, standing alone. I squinted to try and make out exactly what I was looking at and gasped.

A man in a wolf mask.

And he was looking directly at me.

For a moment, I was frozen to the spot, and everything went silent. And then my ears were filled by the deafening roar of the audience. Someone was shaking me.

I broke out of my trance and turned to see the middle-aged gentleman with the Jack Russell holding me by the shoulder and smiling. "Miss! Miss!" he was saying. "You have to go!"

"What?" I said, alarmed and confused.

He pointed at the judge who was standing a few feet ahead, holding a ribbon. "You won, miss! Your bully won!"

Numbly, I stumbled forward with Marge and accepted the ribbon from the smiling judge, who then spun me around to pose for a photo. Once I was released from his grip, I ran with Marge back to the holding area, where Louise and George were waiting. Marge put her paws on Louise's stomach and stood up on two legs while Louise showered her with kisses. "What a good girl!" she crowed.

The owner of the Kerry blue walked by me and shook her head in disgust as she saw the ribbon in Louise's hand. "Congratulations, Lou," she said, again not seeming to mean it.

Louise managed a polite smile until the woman had passed her by, at which point she cackled with delight. "That withered crone has been dogging me for years about how bullies aren't good competitors. Revenge is sweet!"

"Nancy! Congrats!" George said, patting me on

the back. "You did a great job out—hey, is everything okay? You're white as a ghost."

"He was there—in the stands," I said in a low voice. "The man in the wolf mask. We have to find him!"

George's eyes went wide, and after telling Louise we were going to the bathroom, we ran through the big double doors to the stands. I peered out to where I'd seen him sitting, but he was gone.

"Check the exits!" I told George, and we ran off in opposite directions. I looked everywhere. The parking lots were deserted—everyone was still inside, watching the last group of dogs be presented. Finally I gave up and went back inside just in time to meet George, who threw her arms up in defeat.

"Why was he here, do you think?" George asked. "Just to watch you?"

I shrugged. "Or to intimidate me, in case I thought about calling the police."

Just then my phone buzzed in my back pocket, and I pulled it out. A new text message from an unknown number was displayed on the screen.

STOP SNIFFING AROUND AND OBEY, the message read, OR YOUR FRIEND WILL BE PUNISHED.

I resisted the urge to throw the phone across the room and took a deep breath.

George peeked over my shoulder at the message and swallowed hard. "Definitely trying to intimidate you," she said.

"Well, it's not working," I said through gritted teeth. "If anything, it's backfiring. Because we are going to go after Bess. I'm done being obedient. It's time to bite back."

CHAPTER SEVEN

The Oncoming Storm

"ALL BEST IN GROUP WINNERS, PLEASE report to the ring!"

The announcer's voice cut through my thoughts, reminding me that I still had to keep up appearances. If someone working with the smuggler was still hanging around and saw me missing from the winner's circle, it might tip them off to our plans. And anyway, if we were going to rescue Bess, we needed to know where to go.

"Okay," I said to George. "Charles won his group title, so he'll be out there with me. I'll find an opportunity to ask him if he's gotten any news from Interpol about the paper factories. They have to have some information by now."

George nodded. "All right," she said. "And in the meantime—hand over your phone."

I pulled it out of my pocket and gave it to her. "Why do you need it?"

"I want to try and use that text message to see if I can narrow down the location of the phone that sent it. If I use a hack I know, I might be able to triangulate its distance from the nearest cell phone towers—and figure out if someone sent from somewhere in the arena."

"Brilliant," I said, as always amazed by George's technological savvy. "I'll meet you back here as soon as the presentation is over."

I left George and hurried to pick up Marge from Louise so we could join the other winners in the ring. Alice and Pia, Charles and Coco, Joe and Shirley, and Valencia and Hollywood were already there with their ribbons. Helen and Daisy walked out at the same time I did.

"Congratulations!" Helen exclaimed. "Way to go!"

"You too!" I replied.

I found my place in line and turned around to see the final group winner step out into the ring: Angie and Marshmallow Fluff! Angie was beaming when she reached my side, and I leaned over to whisper in her ear. "I guess it will take more than a cruel prank to keep you out of the winner's circle, huh?"

Angie nodded, but a dark look crossed her face. "It's not over, though, Nancy—not by a long shot. There's still the battle for Best in Show tomorrow. Who's to say the saboteur isn't one of the other five people standing out here with us?"

I turned to look at the other winners. Unless Charles was a double agent, which I highly doubted, he was off the suspect list. So that left Alice, Joe, Valencia, and Helen. Given that the jewel smuggler would have to keep winning shows in order to keep up the cover, it was a good guess that they were one of the people in the winner's circle. But was the person who'd drugged Marshmallow also the jewel smuggler? It was possible, but unlikely—why bring unwanted attention to the show? After all, the sabotage was the only reason I'd started investigating at all—if it hadn't happened, the smuggler would have been able to do their business without any trouble. If anything, the incident with Marshmallow put a big crimp in their plans. Knowing that, we probably had not one, but two guilty parties in this group.

"Have you gotten anywhere with your investigation, Nancy?" Angie whispered.

"It's moving along," I said vaguely.

"Well, until you catch whoever did this to my sweet Marshy, I'm going to sleep with the chain on the door and a baseball bat next to my bed!" she said, her eyes narrowed. "Now smile!" She pointed at the crowd, and I smiled as hundreds of cameras flashed while we all posed with our dogs. Hearing the rough edge to her voice, I cast a glance back at Angie. Just because she probably wouldn't drug her own dog didn't mean she couldn't be the smuggler—though it was hard for me to imagine it. But I knew better than to discount a suspect just because I liked them as a person. What if the saboteur was trying to take out a competitor and just happened to mess with the wrong dog? Angie didn't seem like someone who would forgive and forget. She had to stay on the list.

As soon as the pictures were done, I walked over to Charles and Coco. "Congratulations," I said, shaking his hand. And then more quietly, "Any word from Interpol?"

Charles ducked his head close to mine and said, "They're getting close. They think the fibers came either from Papier Nouveau or Lapointe. Both factories have been shut down for a few years and were producing the kind of pulp that those fibers resemble."

"So what are you waiting for?" I asked impatiently. "Bess is in danger!"

"These things take time, Miss Drew," Charles replied. "We need to get confirmation and then a warrant for the current landowner to search the premises. We can't just storm in there, guns drawn! This isn't one of your American action movies."

"Fine," I muttered in frustration. "Your jewel smuggler," I went on. "I have a feeling it's one of the people in the winner's circle."

"I agree," Charles said. "That would fit our profile—vague as it may be. Another reason why my focus needs to be here. The handoff of the jewels is likely to happen at the show—if not today, then tomorrow. We have to find the thief before it's done!" He added, "Your friend's safety is very important to us, mademoiselle, make no mistake. But we're confident she will be safe as long as it appears you aren't digging around. This case spans international borders. We must concentrate our forces on catching the smuggler, or risk losing him again."

"I understand," I said. "Do what you have to do." But like the owner of the Kerry blue, I didn't really mean it.

I considered telling him about the man in the wolf mask and the text message on my phone, but knowing what I was about to do, I didn't want to give Charles any reason to keep me close. If he thought I was in imminent danger, he might put another agent on my tail, and that wouldn't work with my plan—not at all. "You'll let me know as soon as you find out anything more?" I asked.

Charles nodded curtly. "You'll be the first."

I hurried back to the prep area, to drop Marge off with Louise. I forced a smile onto my face and handed over the lead. "She's all yours, Louise," I said. "She'll need to rest up for the big day tomorrow!"

Louise reached out for the lead but grasped my hand instead. Her grip was surprisingly firm. She pulled me in close, bending me down until we were face-to-face. "Now listen, Red," she said, her voice a low growl. "I wasn't born yesterday. Something is going on here—I can see it written all over your face. Does it have to do with who drugged Angie's dog? Do you know who did it?"

I clenched my jaw and looked her straight in the eyes. "Louise," I whispered carefully, "there's more going on here than you know. And I want to tell you about it, but I can't—not yet. But I'll get it sorted out, I promise. You just have to trust me."

Louise backed up, surprised by my answer. "It's trouble, isn't it? Bad trouble?"

I said nothing. But that was enough of an answer for her.

Louise sighed heavily. "I trust you, Red. You're just like your father—always doing the right thing, even if it's the hard thing. But you've got to be careful, do you hear me? If something happens to you . . . your dad would never forgive me."

"I'll be careful," I said. "But for now, I have to go. George and I have something we have to do."

Marge whined at my feet and bumped her head into my hand. I scratched behind her ears. "Keep an eye on your mom, okay, Marge? I'll be back before you know it." And with a wave, I took off to meet George.

As I was walking out to the front of the convention center, a discordant wailing assailed my ears. I found George sitting on a ledge inside near the door, my phone gripped in her hand. Both of our coats, her red parka and my black one, were tossed over her arm.

"What is that noise?" I shouted over the din. "What's going on?"

George looked up and shook her head in dismay. "It's an emergency warning—it goes out to all the phones in the area. There's a huge blizzard coming, Nancy. It's already begun." She gestured out the wall of windows, where snow flurries were swirling through the air, the sky behind a solid wall of slate-gray cloud.

"No . . . ," I moaned. "Not now!"

"If we're going to make it out to find Bess, we've got to go right away. What did Charles say?"

I told George about Interpol narrowing down the locations to two paper factories. "But they're not going to go after her, George—they're too busy trying to track down this smuggler. It's up to us. We have to go it alone."

"But Nancy," George said, casting her gaze around us to check for eavesdroppers. "Do you really think Charles is going to let us go off by ourselves to track her down?"

I took a deep breath and let it out slowly. "What

he doesn't know can't hurt him," I said. "Charles is going to play it by the book—he has to. But by the book might be too late. I'm not willing to wait that long."

George nodded, but I could see a look of fear pass over her face. "For Bess," she murmured.

I squeezed her shoulder. "For Bess."

"And I think I may have a way to figure out which factory she's being held at," George added. "I managed to narrow down the location of the phone that sent that text message to an area of the city—La Cité-Limoilou. If I just check to see if one of those two factories is also in that area . . ." I watched as George pulled up the map on my phone to search for the location of the factories. "Hmm, it looks like Lapointe is south of us, so that can't be right. Now for Papier Nouveau. Wait . . . yes! Nancy, Papier Nouveau is located in the La Cité-Limoilou area of the city! That must be it!"

My heart swelled with the success. "Look out, Interpol," I said, slapping George on the back. "You've got nothing on George Fayne, tech genius."

George handed my phone back to me and zipped up her coat. "Ready to go?" she asked.

I pulled up my hood and pushed my hands into the tight leather gloves I'd brought with me for warmth. "Ready," I said. "Let's go get her."

CHAPTER EIGHT

The Wolf's Den

A BLAST OF FREEZING WIND SLAMMED into my body as the doors to the convention center slid open. George and I stepped out into the swirling maelstrom of snow, pulling our hoods close around our faces. It was late afternoon; I hoped we would find her before dark. I ran out to the street and threw my hand up into the air to hail a passing taxicab. It came to a stop, and the driver rolled down his window.

"We need to get to the La Cité-Limoilou district, quickly!" I said.

The man shook his head. "*Non, mademoiselle—c'est*

impossible. The cabs are not going beyond Old Quebec, not until the storm has passed. You should seek shelter. Stay inside the convention center if you can!"

"Please!" I begged him. "I'll pay you double!"

"Désolé," the driver said. "It's too dangerous!"

"All right," I said. "Just take us as far as you can, then."

The driver nodded, and George and I piled into the back seat. The taxi crawled along the streets, moving painfully slowly through the bumper-to-bumper traffic of people trying to get home before the worst of the blizzard hit the city.

George's leg was tapping impatiently against the floor, and she groaned at every red light. "We could have walked there faster than this!" she muttered under her breath.

"Oh, don't worry, we're going to have to take the last mile or so on foot," I said back. "At least this way we won't be frozen solid by the time we arrive."

"I guess that's true," George said with a sigh, and spent the rest of the cab ride staring out the window at people dashing through the street, many of them carrying bags of last-minute groceries and road salt.

After ten more minutes, the driver pulled over and turned his head to face us. "*Alors*, this is the end of the road, mesdemoiselles. *Bonne chance!*"

I paid him and braced myself for the blast of cold as I opened the door. George and I huddled together at the corner and stared at the map on her phone, trying to find the quickest way to the Papier Nouveau factory. "Follow me!" George shouted over the howling wind, and took off at a jog down the street.

We raced down side streets and through alleyways between buildings, stopping only so George could double-check the map on her phone. The frigid air burned my lungs, but I didn't stop. All around us, the world was getting darker.

Finally, when I felt like I couldn't run another step, I heard George call out, "There!" I stopped and squinted through the falling snow to where she was pointing. I saw a nondescript, squarish white building up ahead, looking a bit dilapidated. Some of the windows around it had broken panes, while others were boarded up, the words DÉFENSE D'ENTRER! written on them in red spray paint. *Keep out.*

Not today, I thought.

"Are you sure this is the place?" I shouted to George.

"Positive!" she answered.

I nodded, and we made our way up to the building. A black sedan and an ATV were the only vehicles parked in the large lot behind the factory, and I went to kneel behind the car, motioning George to follow. "Look," I said, taking a pen from my purse and using it to pry a grayish substance from inside the tire's tread. I removed my glove and rubbed it between my fingers. "It's the same kind of paper fibers we found back at the hotel. I think this is the car they took Bess away in. She's got to be here."

"Wow!" George said, her face brightening with the satisfaction that we'd figured this out on our own. But then her face paled, and she swallowed hard. "Wow...," she said again. And I knew exactly why, because I felt it too. We knew where Bess was being held, but now we had to face the reality of breaking into an abandoned factory in the middle of a blizzard, where at least one potentially armed criminal was standing guard, and we had to do it alone.

"All right," I whispered, my breath visible in the snow-filled air. "Obviously we can't just knock on the door and ask for Bess back with a basket of muffin—"

"Mostly because we don't have any muffins," George cut in.

"Right, right," I agreed. "So we've got to come up with a plan. If we can just get a look inside first, scope out the situation . . ."

"How about there?" George asked. She gestured toward a window on the nearest wall of the factory, which had a few old crates stacked up underneath it. "If we climb up on those boxes, and I put you on my shoulders, you'd be high enough to look through that window."

I nodded. "Let's give it a shot. But we have to be quiet!"

She bent into a crouch, checking all around us

to make sure the coast was clear. A moment later we both ran low across the parking lot, the snow that was accumulating under our feet helping to muffle our footsteps. One at a time, we climbed on top of the pile of big wooden crates. Then, after taking a deep breath, George knelt down, and I clambered onto her shoulders, regretting the large ham sandwich that I'd downed at lunchtime. Luckily, though she was the same size as me, George proved to be as strong as an ox and managed to hoist me up with no problem at all. I grabbed onto the window ledge to steady myself, and rubbed away the condensation on the glass so I could peer inside.

I found myself looking down onto a large open space, with a huge machine taking up most of the length of the factory floor. There were also large metal vats here and there, and piles of discarded paper and garbage moldering in the corners. In the center of the room, under a single bare lightbulb, two men were seated at a card table, playing cards and drinking from steaming paper cups. I scanned the room, craning my neck to see into every dark corner, when finally I saw it. A flash of yellow.

She was sitting on a chair with her ankles tied to the legs. A large cloth was tied tightly around her upper torso and arms so she could use her hands, but not much. As I watched, I could see her trying to wiggle free from her ties, even using her teeth for leverage. Under the blanket they'd put over her shoulders, her blue dress was pretty filthy, but she looked unhurt. Plus, there was a sandwich and a glass of water on the table in front of her. I breathed a small sigh of relief.

Good old Bess!

"I see her," I whispered to George. "She's all right!"

I could feel George's whole body sag with relief under me, and I motioned for her to let me down. We huddled together in a crouch, shielding our faces from the worst of the wind and snow. "There are two of them," I told George. "Sitting at a table playing cards. They're a good distance away from Bess, but one of them is still facing her. She's tied up on a chair near the wall, on the other side there." I sighed. "Even if we snuck in, there's a good chance he'd see us. And we're no good to Bess if we end up captured as well. We need a diversion."

"Describe the rest of the room," George said.

So I told her, in detail, what I'd seen. When I mentioned the massive machine, George's eyes lit up. "The pulping machine," she said. "Do you think it still works?"

"That would depend on whether the factory is still getting power. . . ." I rubbed my chin in thought. "Yes! It must be. They were sitting under a light, and they didn't look like they were freezing to death, so there must still be electricity running through the place. What were you thinking?"

George grinned. "I'm sure that huge, rusty machine suddenly screeching to life would be enough to get their attention, don't you?"

I nodded. "You think you can figure out how to turn it on?" I asked.

"Nancy!" George put her hands up, feigning shock. "Who do you think you're talking to?"

"Oh, all right." I chuckled. "So sorry I ever doubted you!"

Using the clocks on our phones, we planned to wait five minutes before executing the plan. George would sneak in through a back entrance that faced the machine; she was an expert when it came to lock picking, so we had no doubt she would find a way in. Meanwhile I would go through one of the loading bays and make my way to the main room through a hallway that let out near Bess. Once the machine had been activated and the men were distracted, George could escape, I could free Bess, and we could get out together the same way I'd come in.

That was the plan. I wasn't sure if it would work. But I was sure we were going to do it anyway.

Running lightly across the snow-covered ground, I made my way over to the loading bay and climbed the flight of steps into the factory. The place was cold, but the absence of wind made it easier to breathe. It was dark, and mice skittered in the corners as I walked down the empty hallway. I pressed myself up against the wall as I reached the portal into the factory floor, keeping to the shadows. The sounds of voices reached my ears.

"Ach . . . I fold," one of the men was saying. He threw his hand of cards down on the table in disgust, while the other man chuckled and gathered up the stack of coins between them. The first man was lean and had a sharp, angular face and short brown hair that fell in front of his eyes. In any other circumstances, I would have said he was handsome. I guessed he was the charming wolf man from the ball. "If I didn't know better, I'd swear you were counting cards, David."

"Such a sore loser, eh, Jeffrey?" David said. He was a smaller man than his partner, with a short, dark brown beard and a buzz cut. "If I were you," he continued, his voice a threat, "I wouldn't make any accusations that you can't back up with evidence."

I swallowed. Despite the man's size, I could tell that he wasn't someone you messed with. I had to be careful. Really careful.

Jeffrey huffed in disgust. "Just deal the cards," he

spat. As David shuffled, I heard movement from near where I was standing.

"Hey!" Bess called out. "Please, it's been hours. My friends are probably worried sick. Just let me call and tell them I'm all right—even a text would be enough. I know you both have a heart, so please just—"

"Save it," David said, cutting her off. "Rules are rules. No calls, no texts, no nothing—not until Sapphire gives us the okay. Then you're free to go."

Sapphire? I gasped. But I'd thought it was Surefire! Had Interpol had it wrong all this time? My mind whirled with the potential impact this had on the case, but I didn't have time to think about that right now. My phone indicated that the diversion I was waiting for would happen in exactly forty-five seconds. I had to be ready.

"Just keep quiet and eat your sandwich, honey," Jeffrey told Bess. "Going on a hunger strike is only going to make you cranky."

After that comment, I could hear Bess muttering words that made me question my sugary, rose-scented image of her. Clearly, she had had enough.

"We're coming," I whispered to myself, watching the seconds count down.

"I can't wait for this job to be done," Jeffrey said, looking at his new cards. "I'm a thief, not a kidnapper. This whole business with the girl makes me nervous. I don't like it."

"Yes, well—Sapphire doesn't care if you like it or not," David replied. "If we want our share of the money, we do it. Anyway, it will all be over tomorrow. Then you can go and see your superhero movies or whatever. Okay, pal?"

"Listen," Jeffrey said, pointing a finger in his partner's face. "You watch your mouth. I take my superhero movies very seriously."

David sighed heavily and picked through his own hand. "Just hit me, will you?"

"I'm about to," Jeffrey replied, and begrudgingly handed David a card.

The job will be over tomorrow, I thought. *That must mean the handoff of the jewels is happening at the finals of the dog show. I've got to figure out which one of the finalists is Sapphire before the handoff!*

That line of thought was interrupted by a deafeningly loud grinding, screeching sound coming from the factory floor. George had done it!

"What the—?!" David shouted, as he and Jeffrey covered their ears with their hands and jumped up from the card table.

"The machine! Something's triggered it!" Jeffrey yelled over the din. "Quick—turn it off!" The two men ran over to the machine's control panel at the back, and I watched as George, unseen, sneaked back out the door that she'd come in. While the men shouted at each other and pushed buttons, the machine continued to squeal and belch clouds of smoke and paper fibers into the room.

"I'll check the fuse box outside!" David said, running out a back door.

Now was my chance.

I ran low into the room and knelt at Bess's side. "Don't scream," I whispered to her, pulling off the blindfold. "It's me, it's Nancy!"

Bess's blue eyes widened as they focused on me.

"Oh!" she whispered back. "Nancy! Aren't you a sight for sore eyes!"

"C'mon, let's get you out of here," I said, and quickly got to undoing the ropes around her hands. Once those were untied, I started working on the ones around her ankles.

"The ignition key is missing! I can't turn it off!" Jeffrey was bellowing.

Aha, I thought. George must have taken that with her. Good thinking!

"I'm going to go shut off the power to the whole place!" Jeffrey shouted. "It's the only way!" I heard quick footsteps, and then—

"Hey!"

My blood ran cold. We'd been spotted.

The final rope fell away from Bess's ankles, and she leaped to her feet. "Go!" I urged, shoving her toward the hallway that led outside and lurching out after her. "That way! I'm right behind you!"

"Oh, no you're not," said a growling voice behind me, and a strong hand closed around my forearm, jerking me back. I whirled to find myself face-to-face with Jeffrey, his eyes glinting in the dimness of the factory. I tried to pull away, but his grip held firm. "Should have thought twice before wandering into the wolf's den, Little Red. Nothing but trouble to be found here."

CHAPTER NINE

❧

Snowbound

FIGHT OR FLIGHT.

It's the choice we, and all other animals in the world, have to make when faced with a threat. And it's the choice I was facing as I stood in an abandoned warehouse in the middle of a blizzard, my arm in the grip of a criminal, one of the men who'd kidnapped my best friend.

What would he expect me to do? Obviously, he would expect me to run, I thought. To try and wrench my arm away and fly from that place of danger. But if I'd learned anything in all my years of facing down bad guys, it was this: when in doubt, do the unexpected.

Remembering a move I'd learned in a self-defense class, I circled my hand on the arm Jeffrey was holding until I was able to grab his wrist. Then I spun toward him, bringing my elbow up and clocking him across the face.

"Ah!" he cried out, ducking his head away from the blow. I took the opportunity to yank my arm out of his grasp, but before I could take more than a step back, he was lunging at me again, his handsome face red with rage. "Bad move," he muttered. "You'll pay for that."

Clang!

A second later, that face was hit by a large metal pole.

Bess was standing behind him, panting with the effort of lifting the pole and hitting Jeffrey's head with it. Her beautiful blue dress was torn and soiled beyond repair, and her blond hair was sticking out at all angles. She checked to make sure he was still breathing before adding, "That's for ruining my evening," she said. "And don't call me 'honey'!"

"Bess," I said with feeling. "I'm so glad to have you back. Now let's get out of here!"

"Jeffrey, what the heck is going on in here?" another voice said from across the room.

Oh no—David had returned!

The small bearded man looked our way and took off running toward us.

"Go!" I said, and Bess and I ran down the hall and out the door as fast as we could.

The moment we passed through the door, we were hit by a wall of white. Blasts of snow and ice flew into my face and eyes, and a gust of wind blew me almost back into the hallway. "Stay behind me!" I said, hoping to shield Bess from the worst of it. She didn't even have a coat. We tore out into the parking lot and around the building, me leading Bess, half-blinded by the blizzard. "George!" I shouted into the storm. "Where are you?"

For a few terrible seconds, I heard nothing but the winds howling through the building and the trees, but then—the roar of a motor coming to life.

"Over here!" a voice ahead yelled.

I ran toward the sound, and soon George's dark figure came into view, her red coat like a beacon. She was standing astride the ATV that we'd seen parked in the lot when we'd arrived. "Bess!" she exclaimed, and folded her cousin into a tight hug. "I'm so glad you're okay. Here . . ." George began to take off her coat, but Bess stopped her.

"No, you need it just as much as I do," Bess shouted.

"But you'll freeze!" George replied.

"We don't have time to argue!" Bess shouted back. "The kidnappers are coming!"

"How did you get this thing to work?" I asked George.

George smiled. "Left the keys in the storage compartment," she replied. "Classic. I found these, too." She bent down and handed each of us a black helmet, pulling on one for herself.

"Do you know how to drive one of these things?" Bess asked her, adjusting the helmet under her chin.

George shrugged. "How hard could it be?"

Bess and I gave each other a worried look and climbed on behind George. We put Bess in the middle and pressed in close, hoping to keep her protected from the biting cold. While George familiarized herself with the controls, I whipped out my phone and shot a text to Charles: PERPS AT PAPIER NOUVEAU—SEND BACKUP. I prayed that I had enough of a signal during the storm for it to go through.

"Hey! Stop!" came a shout, and through the haze of the storm I could see David and Jeffrey racing through the snow toward us, their faces thunderous with anger.

"Go, George! Floor it!" I shouted.

"I'd love to," George said, "but there's no gas pedal!"

Bess huffed and said, "Put the gear control into drive and release the brake!" She pointed at the various parts of the ATV, and George hastily obeyed. "The throttle is by your right thumb!" George pressed it hard and the ATV shot forward like a bolt of lightning, straight toward a metal Dumpster in front of us. "Turn! Turn!" Bess shouted, and George wrenched the handlebars to the left. The ATV swerved sharply, and

I could feel the whole vehicle start to tip over. "Every-one lean to the left, quickly!" Bess ordered, and we did. The ATV managed to right itself before we all toppled onto the ground with it on top of us.

"How do you know so much about these things?" George spluttered.

"I rode them a lot at the ski lodge with my family," Bess replied, breathless. "I guess I picked up a thing or two. . . ."

"Maybe you should drive," George said, her face pale with shock.

"Maybe I should!" Bess agreed, and clambered to the front. George wrapped her arms around her cousin and Bess hit the throttle just as Jeffrey came running up to us, showering him with a spray of dirty black snow.

"Augh!" he yelled as we sped away.

The ATV raced out of the parking lot and down the empty city streets, the storm buffeting our bod-ies so hard that I had to hold on to George as tightly as I could just to keep from falling off. "Where am I going?" Bess shouted.

"Turn left here!" George replied, pointing at the next intersection. "We have to get back to the Château Frontenac!" We took the corner wide, and Bess pulled back on the throttle to stop us from sliding too much across the snow.

I heard a noise behind me and turned around to see a black sedan lumbering toward us. "Guys!" I called out. "The kidnappers—they're tailing us! We've got to lose them!"

With effort, George pulled her phone out of her pocket and squinted at it, wiping the screen off repeatedly with her sleeve. "Okay . . . Bess, do you think you can manage a sharp right on this thing?"

"I think so," Bess said. "Why?"

"There's an alleyway coming up between those two buildings up ahead." She gestured toward a couple of old row houses with a narrow passageway between them. "If we go through there, it will open up to the main thoroughfare back to the hotel! And the car won't be able to follow us."

"They're gaining!" I shouted as the car revved its

engine and pulled up right behind us. They were close enough that I could see David's and Jeffrey's furious faces in the front seat.

"I'll do my best!" Bess called back to us, and I could see her body tense with concentration. Just as we approached the alleyway, she wrenched the handlebars sharply to the right, and the back of the ATV swung out to the left, skidding along the slippery street. Bess shouted, "Lean to the right! Lean! Lean!" and then turned the handlebars left into the skid. George and I both leaned our bodies to the right, hugging the turn, and the ATV shot into the alleyway, narrowly missing the garbage cans that lined the wall and terrifying a few pigeons into flight.

I turned to see the black sedan screeching to a halt—they hadn't expected us to turn and were trying to compensate. But the car couldn't handle the snow-covered street as well as our ATV could, and I watched as it spun out of control and into a light pole on the corner. David jumped out of the car and banged his fist on the hood as he saw us speeding away.

"I think we're safe for now," I told the girls, and George directed Bess to take the first right out of the alleyway.

"I can see the hotel up ahead!" George called. "We're almost there!"

Bess drove the ATV up the inclined road until finally, we made it under one of the overpasses and found ourselves back in the courtyard of the Château Frontenac. Bess pulled into a parking space and gently applied the brake.

I jumped off the ATV once it came to a stop, my heart hammering with relief and excitement. "Bess, you did it! You got us back!" But she didn't move. She remained where she was, her bare hands gripping the handlebars tightly. Only now did I realize that they were bright red and trembling.

"Bess?" I said, my stomach turning over. "Bess!"

"I'm . . . so . . . cold . . . ," Bess murmured, barely audible in the moaning winds.

"George," I said, tearing off my coat and draping it around Bess's bare shoulders. "We've got to get her inside."

George nodded, her face pale, and helped me uncurl Bess's hands from the handlebars. We each draped one of Bess's arms around our shoulders and carried her between us through the doors to the hotel.

"Help!" I cried out as soon as we got inside. "Someone call an ambulance!"

A concierge ran up to us and looked at Bess's limp, shivering form with alarm. "What happened?" she said.

"She's suffering from exposure," I told her. "Frostbite—we need to warm her up."

The concierge nodded rapidly. "But, mademoiselle, I don't think we can get an ambulance up here in the storm."

"I'm trained in first aid," said Charles, appearing in front of me. I looked up at him and saw that his face was a mixture of frustration and relief. He turned to the concierge. "Get blankets and something warm for her to drink. Hot chocolate—she needs sugar. And some bandages. Quickly!" The concierge nodded and took off down the hallway.

"Sit her down, here." Charles motioned toward a

plushy chair and helped us maneuver Bess into it. "Get her feet elevated. It's her extremities that are in the most danger."

The concierge returned in a few minutes, accompanied by two other hotel attendants, their arms piled with supplies. George knelt by Bess's side and helped her sip the steaming cup of cocoa that they'd brought for her.

Charles pulled me aside. "Mademoiselle Drew," he whispered roughly. "I cannot stress enough how utterly foolish it was of you to launch this reckless rescue mission! You could have been killed!"

"We weren't," I whispered back. "And I wasn't going to wait for Interpol to get around to saving Bess, not when I could do it myself." Charles huffed angrily and rubbed his eyes with his hands. I noticed there were purple circles under them. "Look, I'm sorry if you were worried—but what's important is that we succeeded."

Charles shook his head, muttering to himself. But finally he sighed. "*Alors*, what's done is done. Now tell me everything."

So I described George triangulating the source of the text message, our trip to the paper factory, and all about our run-in with the two kidnappers. Charles asked for their names and asked me to describe them and the car they were driving in detail. Once I was done, he immediately got on the phone with Interpol headquarters in Montreal and gave them all the information. He had already dispatched agents to the paper factory as soon as he received my text message, but just in case the criminals didn't come back there, he wanted to launch a wider search. "Get additional agents out tracking these men right away," he said to the person on the line. "I don't care about the storm. Do it, *maintenant*."

He was about to end the call when I put a hand on his shoulder. "No, wait," I said. "There's one more thing you should know."

"What is it?" he asked, cupping one hand over the phone.

"The jewel smuggler," I said. "The code name isn't 'Surefire'; it's 'Sapphire.' I heard the two kidnappers say it, clear as day."

Charles's eyes widened. "Sapphire," he muttered. "Yes, that makes much more sense for a jewel smuggler, *n'est-ce pas?*"

I nodded. I had been thinking about it myself during the final ride up to the hotel on the ATV. "Not only that," I added, "but I think it's just what we needed to narrow down who the smuggler really is."

Charles cocked his head in curiosity, reminding me very much of his dog, Coco. People really did gravitate toward dogs that resembled them. Another reason why I was pretty sure my hunch was correct. "Oh?" he said with amused curiosity. "Are you going to let me in on your little secret? Or do you plan on trying to catch the criminal yourself as well?"

"No, I think I could use your help on this one," I replied. "But I do have a plan."

Charles chuckled. "Well, I am honored to be invited to your sting operation, Mademoiselle Drew. We have a lot of planning to do before the night is over."

After telling Charles to wait a minute, I went back to see how Bess was doing. She looked much better already and was sitting up and no longer shivering. Her fingers were individually bandaged with soft white gauze, and she was wrapped like a human-size burrito in three or four fuzzy blankets. She looked up at me and smiled as I approached. "Oh, Bess," I breathed. "I'm so glad you're all right."

She nodded. "My fingers and toes are still a little numb, but other than that, I'm no worse for wear. Though I'm starving. What I'd do for poutine!"

"Oh my gosh," George gasped. "A plate of hot, greasy french fries would be amazing right now."

"Are you thinking what I'm thinking?" Bess asked her cousin.

"Room service!" they both said in unison.

"After you stuff yourselves, you both should get some sleep," I said. "I won't be back in the room for an hour or two; I have some things to discuss with Charles. Tomorrow is going to be another big day."

"Oh?" Bess asked. "What's going on?"

"Tomorrow," I told them, "we catch a thief."

CHAPTER TEN

∽

Digging Out the Truth

THE CASE WASN'T SOLVED YET, BUT THAT night I slept much more soundly knowing Bess was safe. George insisted that we all stay in the same room for the night, so Bess and I took the bed, and George made herself comfortable on the sofa with a pile of blankets. They were both still dead to the world when I woke up at seven a.m. to my usual alarm. The sun was still rising as I slipped out of bed and pulled one of the curtains aside. My room had a beautiful view of the snowbound city, where already salt trucks and workers armed with shovels had ventured out to begin clearing the sidewalks and roads. The remnants of last night's storm merely a gray shadow of cloud on the horizon. I watched as members of the hotel staff struggled to dig out some of the cars that were stranded in front of the château, buried under feet of snow. *I have a lot of my own digging to do today,* I thought, and went to make myself a cup of coffee from the little machine on the dresser.

The coffee machine had just started gurgling when there was a knock at the door. George shot up from the couch, throwing off the blankets and looking around blearily. "Ugh," she moaned, stretching. "It's too early for visitors!" I shrugged on one of the thick hotel bathrobes and shuffled toward the door to squint through the peephole. Charles was standing there, looking impatient in a tan suit and paisley tie.

I opened the door, and he immediately walked past me into the room. "I have news," he said.

"Good morning to you, too," George said sarcastically.

"What is it, Charles?" I asked.

"The two thugs who kidnapped Mademoiselle Marvin were apprehended by Interpol last night shortly after you arrived back at the hotel," Charles replied. "They foolishly sped right back to the paper factory after losing you on the street, and my agents were already there waiting for them."

I nodded. It was good to know those guys were off the streets.

"We had hoped to get information about Sapphire from their mobile phones, but unfortunately one of the men smashed his phone before we could get our hands on it. We managed to recover the other man's phone, but the security on it means it will take a while for our people to break through. The good news is that we don't think the men had the opportunity to report back to Sapphire that their hostage had been recovered, or that the men themselves had been arrested. Cell phone signals were spotty last night because of the storm—so it looks as if their calls to the thief never connected. We were lucky to get your text last night, Mademoiselle Drew. So as far as we know, our jewel thief still thinks everything is going according to plan. Where is Mademoiselle Marvin now?"

I pointed to the bed, where Bess was buried under a heap of blankets, still fast asleep. "She's got to be exhausted from the ordeal," I said. "I'd be surprised if she got out of that bed before noon."

"She can stay in bed until tomorrow if she likes," Charles said. "In fact, I recommend it. We want her to remain out of sight until our mission is complete. If Sapphire sees her, the thief will know that the jig is up."

"Okay," I said. "So other than that, it's just like we talked about, right? We go through the finals for the dog show like normal, keeping our eyes open for any signs of who might be there to receive the jewels."

Charles gave a curt nod. "We're fairly certain that the exchange won't happen until after the winner is announced. So we have to close in right before." The coffee machine let out a cheerful *ding!* Charles proceeded to walk over to it and prepare himself a cup, pouring in a serving of creamer and almost too many sugar packets to count. "Any sugar for your cup, Mademoiselle Drew?" he asked, offering her a packet.

"No thank you," I replied.

"Suit yourself. Well, get yourself ready for the day. It's going to be a long one. And remember the most important thing of all—"

"Don't be a hero?" I guessed.

Charles took a sip of his supersweet coffee and grimaced. "Comfortable shoes," he said, and left the room without another word.

"What a strange, strange man," George said after a moment.

"Agreed," I said. "But he's right, we've got to get ready. The show starts in an hour!"

About an hour later, George and I found ourselves scrambling into the convention center with only minutes to spare. The taxicab we'd finally hailed ended up getting stuck in traffic four blocks from the building, so we got out and ran the rest of the way through the snow. Luckily, we had taken Charles's advice and worn our comfortable snow boots! Angie and Alice arrived at the same time as we did in a taxi of their own, and we greeted them both as we approached the entrance.

"Little Alice here hailed a cab for us. Isn't that sweet?" Angie said, patting the younger woman on the shoulder.

Alice blushed and shook her head. "It was nothing," she said.

Inside, Louise was hobbling back and forth on her crutch in the waiting area with Marge, looking frantic. The remaining competitors were standing around with their dogs as the announcer's voice welcomed guests to the show. When Louise saw George and me running in, she clapped a hand against her chest in relief. "Oh! Thank goodness you're here. I thought I was going to have to hobble out into the ring myself. Where have you been?"

"The storm," I said, panting. "Getting here was a challenge."

Louise sniffed. "Where's Bess? Still sick?"

I nodded. "Getting better, though."

Louise shook her head. "Must be something going around—I heard there was some kind of medical emergency in the hotel lobby last night. No one would give me any details, though. Do you girls know what happened?"

George and I looked at each other and shrugged.

"Oh, well. Anyway—come on, ladies! It's showtime! The big day is upon us!"

I gulped and followed Louise toward the ring's entrance. Unlike the day before, I didn't have time to be nervous, because the moment I got to the front of the crowd, I heard the announcer say, "And now, for our first finalist—the winner in the Terrier Group. Please welcome Marge the bull terrier, and her handler, Miss Nancy Drew!" A moment later Louise shoved Marge's lead into my hand and George propelled me out into the bright light of the arena. I stood frozen for a moment, staring out into the crowds of people in the stands and the table of expectant-looking judges, still trying to catch my breath. Something wet on my hand made me look down to see Marge nuzzling me and gazing up at me with her little black eyes.

"Thanks for the pep talk," I whispered to her. "Let's do this!"

I relaxed my shoulders and smiled at the crowd, who welcomed us to the ring with a round of applause. We did our circuit, the same as yesterday, and then stopped to stand for the judges. One of them, a bald man with tiny circular glasses, examined Marge from top to bottom but seemed distracted as he did it, which struck me as strange. His eyes kept flicking toward the waiting area, and I noticed one of his hands tapping nervously on his leg. Could this man be Sapphire's buyer? It was worth keeping in mind.

After a few minutes, the judge declared that he was done and released us back to the waiting area. Louise welcomed us with open arms. "You did great!" she announced. "You made it, Red—now all you have to do is sit back and wait for the results."

I spied George sitting nearby and collapsed into a

chair next to her. "See anything interesting while I was out there?" I murmured in her ear.

"Mmm," George replied, nibbling on her fingernails. She always kept them short, but when she was anxious, she had a bad habit of biting them to the quick. "Well, most of them look pretty nervous, I'd say. Joe hasn't stopped pacing the room since you left. The only ones who seem to be holding up well are Valencia and Helen. Both of them have just been sitting there on their phones—V seems to be taking more selfies with her dog, and Helen has been texting nonstop, with her kids and husband, probably. That's all she ever talks about."

I sighed. "It could go either way," I said. "It could be that the thief is nervous because they know that the exchange is about to happen, or they could be the kind of person who's done this so many times that it's a cinch."

"But I thought you knew who the thief was—not that you've told me."

"I have a hunch," I admitted. "But I won't know for sure if I'm right until we set the trap."

George looked at me. "What if you're wrong? I mean, this person could be dangerous, right?"

I looked out at the small group of people still waiting to show their dogs. Joe, Valencia, Alice, Helen, and Angie. None of them looked dangerous. But one of them was.

"Let's just hope I'm not wrong," I said.

Half an hour later, once all the dogs had their turns, the other competitors and I retired to a back room to wait for the judges' decision. It was a fairly large room, with a dozen chairs, a table covered in magazines about Quebec City, and a mini fridge filled with bottled water. I downed an entire bottle of water, and then poured half of another into a little cup for Marge. She lapped it up gratefully, and then looked at me and whined. It was almost as if even she knew that something big was about to happen.

Helen was seated on the small sofa, telling Valencia all about her fashion collar business, and Joe was pacing. Alice was sitting alone with Pia in her arms, not saying anything to anybody. Angie went over to her and offered her a mint. "Uh, no thank you," Alice said, waving her hand at the tin. Angie shrugged and popped a few into her own mouth before picking up a magazine. She didn't seem very nervous—despite the setbacks Marshmallow had experienced. Charles and Coco came in last, and he closed the door behind him with a distinctive *click*. Our eyes met, and he gave me a subtle nod.

It was time.

I took a deep breath, then stood up and cleared my throat. Like a bunch of English pointers, everyone's heads turned immediately to look at me. The dogs, however, looked bored. All of them except for Daisy, who was watching me attentively. But then again, Daisy was a Doberman, so that might just come with the territory. I handed Marge's lead to Angie, who took it with a look of confusion. "Like the rest of you," I began, taking a few steps into the center of the room, "I've been working hard to give my dog a shot at the big prize. But I've been working on something else, too.

I've been trying to find out who drugged Marshmallow Fluff and sabotaged her chances at the show."

Everyone looked at one another uncomfortably. This probably wasn't news to anyone, but having it said out loud made it all too clear what was about to happen. Angie tightened her grip on Marshmallow's lead, and Charles crossed his arms. "So for the past couple of days, I've been watching all of you very closely. And I've noticed quite a few strange things going on. Some of you in this room, I think, aren't what you seem."

At those words, Joe Cook slammed his fist down on the table, making the pile of magazines—and half the people in the room—jump. "I knew I couldn't get away with it," he muttered. Helen gasped.

I swallowed. "Get away with what, Joe?"

"I figure you know what, so why don't you tell them?" Joe said irritably.

"I don't—" I started to say.

"Oh, don't toy with me," he sputtered. "Just tell them that my name is really José Columbo! That I'm really a pro wrestler under the name Bull's-Eye!"

Angie's jaw dropped. "I knew I'd seen him some-where before!"

Joe sighed, his enormous shoulders slumping. "If the other wrestlers or the federation knew that I showed dogs in my spare time, I'd never hear the end of it. So when I got Shirley, I decided that when I was on the road with her, I'd have a new identity. That way no one would know. But I guess it didn't work, after all."

"Ohh," I breathed. "So that's why you paid off that guy in the alley when he recognized you. You didn't want him giving away the secret."

Joe nodded. "You saw that, huh? Figures. Look, I just wanted to Shirley to be the star—not me. I wanted her to win because she's beautiful, my little heart-breaker." Joe hefted the dog like a baby doll and kissed her on the nose. "But I never hurt Angie's dog," he said with passion. "No way. I love dogs more than I love winning. I wouldn't hurt a fly. Unless it was in the ring, of course."

"I know, Joe," I said. "Really, I didn't even know all that stuff about the wrestling."

Joe blushed. "So . . . I just outed myself for no reason?"

"Looks like it," I replied.

"Oh," he said, leaning back in his chair.

"No," I continued. "I had an idea of who had drugged Marshmallow once I'd gotten a whiff of Valencia's chewing gum in the elevator."

Valencia's eyes, heavy with liner and mascara, widened like a couple of Venus flytraps. "Be careful where you tread, Nancy," she growled.

I glanced at her, unfazed, and went on. "The gum that was used on Marshmallow was bubble-gum flavor, but Valencia only chews cherry-flavored gum—her breath always smells of it. It was an oversight clearly made by someone looking to pin the crime on another person, and why not Valencia? She's passionate, competitive—people would easily believe she was capable of something like that."

Valencia stood up. "Hey! What are you saying?"

"I'm saying you're innocent," I replied, crossing my arms.

Valencia looked confused. "Oh," she said, slowly sitting back down.

"Now, any one of you had a motive to pull this stunt," I said. "By ruining Marshmallow's fur, you'd be removing her from the competition, and if Valencia was accused of the crime, then Hollywood Garden would be out of the running too. Two birds with one stone." I paused. "But one of you made the mistake of calling attention to yourself, when you pointed the finger at Valencia."

At that moment, Alice, who had been sitting stock-still this entire time, burst into tears.

Angie looked over at her, shocked. "Alice?" she said. "You? But—"

"I'm so sorry!" Alice finally managed. "Pia really needed this one to move to the next level, and I was worried that Marshmallow was a favorite. I was never going to hurt her; I just wanted her out of the way. But as soon as it was done, and I saw how upset you were . . . I felt awful! I wanted to take it all back. But it was too late."

I walked over and put a hand on her shoulder. "Alice," I said softly, "it's never too late to do the right thing."

Alice buried her face in her hands. "I'm sorry," she said again.

"Well," said Valencia, picking up her phone again, "I'm glad that's over."

I held up a hand. "Not quite," I said.

Valencia licked her red lips and trained her eyes on me.

"You see, what I didn't realize at first was that there was something much more sinister going on at this dog show, and that my sniffing around about the attack on Marshmallow made the person behind it all very, very nervous. So nervous, in fact, that they resorted to extreme measures to try and stop my investigation."

"What in the world are you talking about, Nancy?" Joe asked.

"I'm talking about an international jewel smuggler disguising themselves as a dog show exhibitor," I answered. "And using these competitions as a front to exchange stolen jewels for money."

Everyone in the room except for Charles gasped. Helen—who had spent almost this entire time looking down at her phone—looked up abruptly, her blue eyes round.

"You've got to be kidding," Angie said.

"I wish I was," I said. "But if you don't believe me, you can ask Charles—he's an undercover Interpol agent. He's been trying to catch this smuggler for a long time."

Everyone's heads turned to look at Charles, who rewarded them with a slight grin and a crisp bow.

"This smuggler was so threatened by my presence," I continued, "that they had their thugs kidnap my friend Bess from the masquerade ball two nights ago."

Another gasp from the room.

"They said that they'd release Bess only if I stopped sniffing around. But I didn't stop, and I also didn't wait for them to let her go. What the smuggler doesn't know is that not only did we already rescue Bess last night, but both accomplices have been apprehended by Interpol."

At that, there was a clatter. I looked around and saw that Helen's cell phone had fallen to the floor. I caught a glimpse of the screen before it shut off—a chat window with someone named Jeffrey.

"He's not going to answer you, Helen," I said, slowly. "Or should I say, Sapphire?"

Helen bent to retrieve her phone from the floor, got up to press the wrinkles from her slacks, and pushed a stray lock of hair carefully behind her ear. "Well, Nancy," she said, her honeyed voice dripping with malice. "Aren't you a clever girl?"

"If I've learned anything from being in this dog show," I said, "it's that people are a lot like their dogs. Dobermans are brilliant, aggressive dogs. Dogs you wouldn't want to mess around with. Kind of like you. Right, Helen?"

Daisy sat up at attention as Helen rose to her feet. "You know, you're right. Daisy and I do have a lot in common." she said. "Not only does she put on a good show, she's a fabulous attack dog too." Helen then unbuckled Daisy's collar and tucked it into her purse. She walked over to the door and threw it open. Before fleeing, she turned, pointed to me, and shouted, "Daisy! Attack!"

The Doberman's lip curled as a menacing growl started deep in her throat. Before I could make a single move, she took a step toward me, teeth bared.

CHAPTER ELEVEN

Collared

THE SECONDS PASSED LIKE MINUTES AS I stood, staring into Daisy's dark eyes, waiting for her to attack. Helen had run out the door and was gone. Everyone else in the room was rooted to the spot, afraid that any movement would only make the big dog lash out at them, too. Even the other dogs looked scared—Pia the shih tzu was trembling in Alice's arms, and Shirley the basset hound's expression was even more worried than usual.

I knew I had mere moments before the Doberman leaped on me, just as her owner had commanded her to. I had to think fast. But what could I do?

I didn't have anything to defend myself with. I'd left my bag with George when I had to do the show with Marge. All I had in my pockets was what I needed to be her handler—

That's it, I thought.

All I had was all I needed.

Trying to move as slowly as possible, I reached into my pocket and found the little plastic clicker Louise had given me to help work with Marge. I quickly pressed the button, which emitted two loud, tonal clicks. For a second, Daisy's growl faltered and she cocked her head. She was confused—she was about to attack me, but I was using a signal that signified that a treat was coming. It distracted her for only an instant, but that was enough.

"José," I called out to the wrestler. "Take her down! Now!"

In a flash, the huge man got a running start and slid on his knees toward Daisy. Before the Doberman knew what was happening, José had locked his strong arms in a seat-belt grip over the dog's one shoulder and under the other arm before pulling her up and into his lap. The dog's arms and legs flailed in the air, and she growled and barked furiously, trying to turn her head enough to bite her attacker. But José was able to keep his chin tucked tight to her shoulder and out of harm's way. "Shhhh," he cooed at the furious dog, who, despite her size, looked like a puppy in his enormous arms. "It's gonna be okay," he said. "Just calm down, little girl."

I shook my head in disbelief and ran over to Charles, who was already on the phone, calling for backup from Interpol. "All agents—perp is on the run. Monitor all exits and apprehend on sight," he was saying. When he saw me run up, he pulled the phone away from his face. "Mademoiselle, are you all right?" he asked.

"Yes, yes, I'm fine," I said impatiently. "Which way did she go?"

"You must be very pleased," Charles continued, ignoring my question. "Your hunch was correct."

"Charles!" I exclaimed. "Tell me where she went!"

Charles reached out and grabbed me by the

shoulders. "Mademoiselle Drew, the situation is under control. There is no way that Madame Sapphire can escape—my agents have every door covered and are swarming the place as we speak. In mere moments, she will be in our custody. It's over."

I shook my head. "No," I said, thinking about how I'd felt when Bess was in danger. "I'm seeing this one to the end." Running over to Angie, I took Marge's lead back from her and sped from the room, the bull terrier running obediently by my side. A crowd of showgoers was milling around outside the door, and I struggled to push my way through them, craning my neck for a glimpse of Helen. Suddenly a hand grabbed my arm and I whirled around—but it was just Louise.

"Nancy!" she said. "Is everything okay? You're as white as a ghost!"

"Have you seen Helen?" I asked quickly. "Helen Bradley—have you seen her?"

Louise crinkled her brows and said, "Hmm, I might have seen her on the way up to the balcony a minute ago. Looked like she was in an awful hurry.

Can't imagine why . . ." I started to take off toward the stairs when Louise stopped me. "Hey now, slow down, Red! Why in the world are you chasing Helen Bradley?"

I took a deep breath. "She's an international jewel smuggler trying to escape from Interpol," I said all at once.

Louise blinked twice. "Oh," she said.

"I'll explain later!" I said, and handed Marge's leash to her.

"No—take her with you," Louise urged, handing me Marge's lead and nudging the dog toward me. "You never know when you might need a little extra muscle."

I nodded and motioned for the bull terrier to follow. Marge and I pushed through the crowd and made our way to the stairs. We took the steps two at a time. When we got to the balcony, which curved around the back half of the stage and looked down on the ring below, it looked deserted. The guests must have all still been downstairs getting refreshments before the big winner was announced. I took a few steps forward, peering down the aisles, to see if someone might be hiding there, but saw nothing out of the ordinary. Could Louise have been mistaken about seeing Helen go this way?

I turned around to head back downstairs and pulled on Marge's lead, but she didn't budge. I pulled a little harder and was about to call the dog's name, but then I noticed how still Marge was. She was standing at attention, as if she were being examined by one of the judges, and her eyes were focused on a single point in the distance. Silently, I followed her gaze to a pillar near the far end of the balcony. A pillar just wide enough to conceal a person behind it.

Swallowing hard, I began walking toward the pillar, taking one careful step at a time. "Helen," I called out, "I know you're there. You're going to have to give up now—Interpol has the place locked down."

There was a pause, and then a chuckle. "You think this is the worst situation I've been in?" a voice finally said. "Not even close. Although you certainly have made things difficult for me. I quite enjoyed being sweet, darling Helen Bradley. I suppose now I'll have to come up with something else. Maybe a brunette this time . . ." Helen's voice trailed off. But then she asked, "Just out of curiosity, how did you know?"

I took a couple more steps. "It was a lot of little things, really," I said. "You were there when Louise first asked me to investigate the matter with Marshmallow—so if you'd overheard the conversation, you'd have been one of the first people who knew I was even a detective. Then later, Valencia told me you'd gotten Best in Show in Helsinki, and I remembered that Charles had said that Finland was the last place he'd been investigating in the case. Then, after Bess was kidnapped, you were the only one who specifically asked about her the first day of the show. It was meant to look like interest and concern—but you were really just checking to make sure I would lie about what was really going on, that I was holding up my end of the bargain and keeping my mouth shut."

"And all the while you were planning on breaking into my hideout yourself," Helen said. "Hunting the hunter, eh, Nancy? Very clever."

"Cleverer than those two goons you had working for you," I said. "It was them you were texting all those times on your phone—not your husband and kids. Actually, it was that phone of yours that finally clinched it for me."

"Oh? How so?" Helen asked.

"When we first ran into you on the street, I got a glimpse of the background on your phone—a picture of your so-called family and Daisy. But although I've never seen your husband and kids, I did see your dog after that. And the dog in that picture isn't Daisy, is it? Daisy has two tan spots above her eyes—very distinctive markings. The dog in the picture doesn't. It's a stock photo. I even found it online." I was so close now, only a few feet away.

"You're starting to annoy me, Nancy." Helen's voice had been playful before, but now all hints of pleasantness were gone. "I don't appreciate you taking apart all my carefully laid plans. I don't think you're a very nice girl."

"You think that everyone else is too stupid to look

closely at you," I said, still moving forward. "That no one would expect someone who looks like an innocent suburban mom to be a criminal. So you got cocky. You even gave yourself a code name that gives the game away. Not only the name of a pretty jewel, but also the color of your eyes—"

I took one last step toward the pillar and saw Helen's furious face peering out at me from behind it.

"Sapphire."

With a cry of rage, Helen leaped out of her hiding place and ran at me. The attack took me a little by surprise, but I had just enough time to brace myself in a defensive crouch. Helen tackled me and tried to pull me to the ground, but I kept my elbows tight to my chest and my hands up, so she wasn't able to get a good grip. When her initial attack failed, she then got low and wrapped her arms around my waist, driving me backward toward the balcony railing. My breath started coming in quick gasps as I realized how low the railing was, and how high up we were. Dimly, I heard the sound of barking, but it was hard to hear anything over the sound of my heart roaring in my ears. With a grunt, I pushed down on Helen's head and splayed my legs back out to try and get back some of my balance and keep her from pushing me any nearer to the railing. But Helen's anger had given her strength, and despite all my efforts, we were still inching closer and closer to the edge.

And then—a miracle.

"Stop! Police! Put your hands where we can see them!"

I lifted my eyes to see Charles flanked by three uniformed officers, and none other than the intrepid Marge standing at his feet, her tail wagging.

Helen looked up too, and at the sight of the Interpol agents, all the fight went out of her. She let go of me and sagged into one of the front-row seats in the balcony, looking out at the ring below. "Well," she said with a sigh. "It was a good run while it lasted."

Charles rushed up and ordered the other officers to put Helen in handcuffs and read her rights to her. Marge trotted up to me and licked my hand. "You ran off once Helen jumped out at me, didn't you?" I said to the dog. "You went to get help. Good girl!" I scratched her behind her ears, and her little eyes squeezed shut with pleasure.

"Mademoiselle Drew," Charles said, walking up to me with his hands on his hips. "If I was not so pleased that this criminal has finally been apprehended, I would have half a mind to call your father. Do you always insist on being so outrageously reckless?"

I cocked my head. "Possibly—but then again, I've been in worse spots than this. And besides, if you called my father, he'd probably tell you to pat me on the back and give me a medal."

Charles shook his head. "I know Americans are crazy, but you, mademoiselle, you are in a league of your own."

"Thank you," I said with a smile. "I'll take that as a compliment."

We followed the officers and Helen back down to the first floor, where George and Louise were waiting, looking a bit frantic. When they saw me, they both rushed over. "Red!" Louise exclaimed. "Good gracious, what is going on? Interpol? International jewel smugglers? This is a dog show, not a James Bond movie!"

I blushed. "I'm sorry, Louise. I promise I'll explain everything later, but for now, suffice it to say that Bess got kidnapped, George and I rescued her, Alice drugged Marshmallow Fluff and feels really bad about it, Joe is really a famous professional wrestler, Charles is a secret agent, and Helen is a wanted criminal."

With every word, Louise's eyes got bigger and bigger, and her jaw dropped just a little more. A moment later I saw several more officers coming toward us, holding a very panicked-looking man who was also in handcuffs. I recognized him immediately: the distracted judge. "So he was the buyer!" I said to Charles. "I thought he might be."

Charles nodded. "He came up to us carrying a suitcase full of cash. Figured he was going to get caught and was hoping to buy himself some goodwill. The only missing piece is the jewels themselves. We've already gone through all of Helen's bags and belongings and haven't been able to find a thing."

"Hmm," I said, mulling over a couple of small details in my mind. "I might just be able to help you with that, too." I walked over to the officers, who had Helen seated in a chair while they filled out some paperwork. "Did you happen to find a dog collar with her? Bright blue and leather?" The officers dug through Helen's handbag and fished out Daisy's collar, which Helen had removed before running off. At first I'd just thought she was doing it to let Daisy loose, but what if it was more than that? As it was hand-made, it wasn't just a flat collar like many of the other dogs wore, but was made of leather folded over on itself and stitched shut. I examined the buckle and saw that it was shoved into the leather—not glued or stitched. Slowly I wiggled the buckle free, exposing the hollow inner core of the collar.

"Mon Dieu . . . ," Charles whispered as I shook the collar, and a cascade of glittering diamonds, rubies, and sapphires came pouring out into my hand.

"The jewels were never on Helen's person at all," I said, piecing it together. "That's how she got everything through customs. They were always hidden with Daisy. And no one ever thought to check the dog."

Charles took the jewels from me and grinned. "Perhaps I will call your father after all," he said. "I'd like to ask him if he would consider allowing you to stay here in Quebec permanently. You could have a bright future waiting for you at Interpol!"

"Hey!" George cut in. "Nancy's got her hands full back in River Heights. If you want her for another case, you're going to have to fly us all back here for it—all expenses paid. And I expect a lot of poutine."

Charles and I laughed. Then the voice of the announcer boomed over the noise of the crowd. "Attention! The judges have made their decision. Please make your way back to your seats for the announcement of the Best in Show!"

CHAPTER TWELVE

Every Dog Has Her Day

WITH ONE LESS DOG AND ONE LESS JUDGE in the ring, there was a bit of confusion in the stands, where news of the arrest was spreading like wildfire. *"Silence, s'il vous plaît!"* the announcer was saying for the third time. Finally the noise in the crowd died down, and one of the remaining two judges got up to approach the line of finalists. It was Alice and Pia, José and Shirley, Charles and Coco, Valencia and Hollywood, Angie and Marshmallow, and me and Marge at the end. Helen had been taken away by the Interpol agents, and Daisy was being attended to by a couple of the show assistants, who'd been feeding her dog biscuits when we left them. Apparently, soon after José had tackled her, she'd given up the fight and had been as docile as a puppy ever since.

"What do you think is going to happen to Daisy after all this is over?" I whispered to Angie.

She shrugged. "No idea. She's not a bad sort—just been taught a few naughty tricks. Her owner certainly belongs behind bars, but that poor dog didn't do anything to deserve the same treatment."

I nodded. "I'm sure she'll be able to find a new home—a beautiful dog like that? Oh! The judge . . ." I quickly stood at attention and had Marge do the same. The judge, a petite woman with short black hair and almond-shaped eyes, had reached us and was standing before the line of dogs and handlers. In her hand was a large purple-and-gold ribbon. Seeing that the announcement of the winner was imminent, the rowdy audience went dead silent.

"Here we go," I heard Angie whisper. I watched as she closed her eyes and muttered a silent prayer, one hand on Marshmallow Fluff's furry head, the other on her heart.

"First," the judge spoke into her microphone, her voice amplified throughout the arena, "I'd like to thank you all for a wonderful exhibition. Despite the, uh, unexpected developments, you have all handled this competition with skill and pride. We had fine choices in each breed, but at the end of the day, one dog rose above the rest to become the next Best in Show! And that dog is . . ."

Everyone seemed to hold their breath in that moment. Who would it be?

"Our Old English sheepdog—Marshmallow Fluff!"

The entire crowd exploded in cheers as the judge handed the ribbon to Angie, who was paralyzed with shock. "Angie!" I shouted, grabbing her hands. "You did it! You won!"

After a few seconds, Angie seemed to snap out of her daze and began to scream and jump up and down, hugging the ribbon to her chest. Wanting to join in on the excitement, Marshmallow started jumping and barking and trying desperately to lick anyone who was close enough to her mouth. That included Angie, me, and the judge.

"Oh, Marshmallow! No! Off!" Angie cried.

Luckily, the judge seemed to have a sense of humor. She laughed and gave Marshmallow a rub behind the ears. "She's just celebrating," the judge said, chuckling.

"Thank you," Angie said to the judge, her eyes glassy with tears. The judge nodded and went to greet the other finalists.

"Congratulations, Angie," a small voice said. Angie and I looked to see Alice standing there, holding on to Pia as if the little dog would give her the courage to speak. "I just wanted to say again that I'm so sorry for all the trouble I caused. I'll never do anything like that again . . . I just feel terrible."

The young woman started to turn away, but Angie stopped her. "Alice," she said, laying a hand on her arm. "I forgive you."

Alice squeezed her eyes shut, and then sighed. "Thank you," she whispered.

Marshmallow Fluff walked over and head-butted Alice's leg affectionately. "It looks like Marshmallow forgives you too," Angie added.

A little while later, all the finalists and their friends and family were gathered at Canard Mauve, a beautiful French bistro deep in Quebec City's historic district. The restaurant was located in a lovely old building with all its original dark woodwork, the walls decorated with dozens of paintings by different local artists. Each painting, I realized, included a little purple duck—which was how the bistro got its name. The room was full of people and cheerful noise, and I was sitting with my two best friends at a table near the front window. Outside, the snow-covered city looked like a postcard, the sun setting spectacularly over the water in an explosion of purples and pinks.

Bess, who was thrilled to finally be able to leave her hotel room, had dressed in a flowy brown skirt and emerald-green blouse for the occasion, with a string of wooden beads around her neck. It made me feel good to see her this way—happy and looking like herself again. She was drinking hot apple cider with George, who had finally gotten her hands on another plate of poutine.

"Oh man," George was saying, in between bites. "I never want to stop eating this stuff."

Bess eyeballed the already half-empty plate and shook her head. "You keep going like that, we're going to have to roll you out of this place."

"I don't care," George replied. "More, I say, more! Poutine forever!"

I laughed and turned to Louise. She was nursing a ginger ale and petting Marge, who was almost as interested in George's poutine as George was. "I'm really sorry Marge didn't win, Louise," I said.

"Oh, there's always another show," Louise said, waving away my apology. "Besides, Angie deserved this one. She's been working hard for years—it was her moment to shine."

I glanced over to the center of the room, where Angie was posing for pictures with Marshmallow

Fluff, who was proudly wearing her Best in Show ribbon around her neck. Angie was positively glowing.

"Oh, and guess what?" Louise went on. "José Columbo says he's going to adopt Daisy! She and Shirley apparently got on very well during the show, and he's been wanting to get her a companion for a long time. Isn't that nice?"

I nodded. "Good for Daisy. She's a perfect dog for a pro wrestler. She already knows some of the moves!"

A moment later Charles stood up on a chair, a glass of wine in his hand. *"Mesdemoiselles et messieurs!"* he said loudly. "May I have your attention for a moment, *s'il vous plaît?"* The crowd quieted down, and Charles cleared his throat. "I have done quite a few exciting dog shows over the past couple of years," he began, "but this one takes the cake!" Everyone laughed. *"Alors,* as many of you now know, there was a criminal in your midst, someone I had been unsuccessfully tracking with Interpol for a long time. If it had not been for the ingenious—and may I say, extremely ill-advised!— work of these three young women"—Charles gestured toward me and the girls—"that criminal may have gone free once again. And so I must ask you all to please give these gutsy Americans a round of applause!"

Everyone clapped, and Louise hooted loudly. Bess's cheeks turned beet red, and she smiled shyly while George grinned happily. Charles waved me over to speak, bidding me to stand on a chair beside him. "Thank you," I said as the applause ended. "Other than the kidnapping, the car chase, and the blizzard, this actually has been a very pleasant vacation," I joked. "But before we all take a drink, I'd like to dedicate this toast to the real hero of this story, whose bravery and quick thinking ended up saving the day, and who really has a nose for detective work. Here's to you, Marge!"

Upon hearing her name, the bull terrier sat up and barked, her tail wagging.

Everyone raised their glasses and shouted, "To Marge!"

Dear Diary,

WELL, IT SEEMS AS IF MY PLANS FOR relaxing and getting away from it all went to the dogs! Who'd have thought that a petty little prank would lead me into the world of international crime? Luckily, despite everything that happened these past few days, the girls and I ended up having a great time. We even got a picture with Bonhomme in the ice palace! Before we had to get our flight home, Louise presented each of us with a gift. She gave George a Quebecois recipe book (homemade poutine, here she comes!) and Bess a canister of the region's best cocoa mix. My present was a framed photo of Marge and me taken at the competition. I'll cherish it forever. After all, that pup and I made a great team!

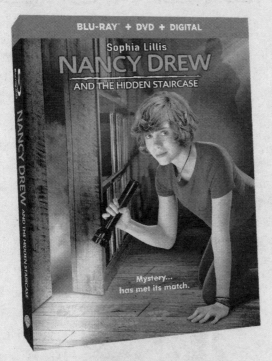

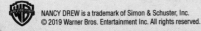

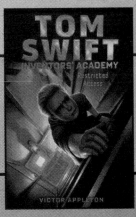

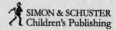 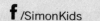